"We could have had a real date tonight."

Seth leaned against Jassy's trailer as he spoke.

Jassy stared at him. His silver-tipped dark hair was tied back with a strip of leather. He looked a little wild. Exciting. And dangerous.

"I thought we *were* on a date," she said recklessly. She could handle him. "But you sure have a crummy way of saying good-night."

"I haven't said good-night at all," Seth muttered, pulling her gently to him.

Jassy's heart flip-flopped. The kiss started slow and soft. His tongue caressed her lips, then invaded her mouth. She shivered as his arousal pressed against her. She wanted him more than she'd ever dreamed possible.

And one thing was shockingly clear . . . Jassy couldn't handle Seth at all.

Lynn Patrick is the pseudonym for the writing team of Patricia Pinianski and Linda Sweeney. The Chicago-based duo are both concerned about endangered species and set out to dispel some of the popularly held myths about wolves. In *Wild Thing*, their first Temptation novel, Linda and Pat have created a dramatic tale in which their fondness and regard for animals and the wilderness are evident. Enjoy!

Books by Lynn Patrick

Wild Thing

LYNN PATRICK

Harlequin Books

TORONTO • NEW YORK • LONDON
AMSTERDAM • PARIS • SYDNEY • HAMBURG
STOCKHOLM • ATHENS • TOKYO • MILAN
MADRID • WARSAW • BUDAPEST • AUCKLAND

Published May 1992

ISBN 0-373-25495-4

WILD THING

1

"A-A-W-OO-O-O . . ."

A plaintive cry pierced the summer-morning quiet
and a chill shot down Jassy Reed's spine. The mourn-
ful lament stirred her as did everything about the rug-
ged, stunning Northwest Coast. Gasoline splashing
onto her boot roused her to release the hose's trigger.

"A-a-w-oo-o-o . . ."

"Oo-o-h-h . . ."

"A-a-w-w-w . . ."

There it was again—an inhuman voice—this time
joined by several others, each at a different pitch yet
blending in a strangely pleasing melodic disharmony.
Goose bumps prickled along Jassy's arms and the
breath caught in her throat. Lonely dogs?

Or wolves?

Jassy grinned, screwed down the gasoline cap and
hung up the hose. The idea of a wolf chorus appealed
to her. It suited these forested mountains. Minal was a
small town at the edge of civilization and nestled
against Washington's Olympic National Forest. She
pictured herself in the wilderness where the magnifi-
cent creatures once roamed free among the centuries-

old black cottonwoods, red cedar and western hemlock.

The picture quickly faded. Jassy figured the wolf had long ago been eradicated from the Peninsula as in most of the country.

The howling faded away....

A familiar chill of loneliness swept through her. Ignoring it, she approached the wizened old codger who stood in the open doorway of the weathered, ramshackle gas station. He wore faded, patched overalls and a plaid shirt that seemed thin from too much washing. His expression was closed, formidable. Jassy smiled and, reluctantly, she thought, he tipped his cap before taking her money.

"Mornin'," he grunted.

"It's a wonderful morning, isn't it?" Unable to contain her enthusiasm for a new day, a new adventure, she tilted her face to the rising sun and breathed deeply of the fresh, cool air.

"Better 'n a lot of days, anyways." He seemed wary of her exhilaration. With an arthritic hand he held out her change. "These bones are too old to take the chill and damp we usually get in May."

Jassy enveloped his gnarled fingers with both her hands in a comforting gesture. "Then I'm glad it'll be a good day for you." She slid the change into her jacket pocket.

He suddenly smiled back at her, revealing broken teeth. "You're a right perky young lady," he stated. "Not from these parts."

"No. But I was thinking about sticking around for a while, if I can find a job. Do you know of any?"

"Nope."

Jassy was disappointed, but she wasn't about to lose heart so easily.

"Leastwise nothing but a grunt job," he added. "Hard, dirty work. You don't look like no hired man to me."

"I can be a hired man." She'd done her share of physical labor over the past several years; she could bluff her way through anything she hadn't tried before. Acquaintances thought she was crazy for leading such a nomadic life, but she liked it. "Where?" she demanded. "Who do I talk to?"

The man laughed. "You sure are all-fired enthusiastic." Squinting, he gave her dusty leathers a once-over and chuckled. "And you look pretty tough—for a little thing. Wouldn't *he* have an eyeful."

"He who?"

"Seth Heller. Runs a refuge called Wolf's Lair."

She whipped around to face southeast, the direction from which the haunting sounds had come. "I wasn't imagining it?"

"Them howls was for real, all right."

"How do I get there?" She couldn't hide her excitement.

"You're set on being a hired man, are you?" His smile faded. "But I don't think you want *this* job—working for the likes of him."

"Oh, come on. I can take care of myself. And after I get the job, I'll buy all my gas at your station," she joked, knowing his was the only one for miles.

He chuckled. "How can I turn down a new customer? Name's Whit Bickel."

"Jassy Reed." She zipped up her black leather jacket.

"Go back the way you came about a mile," he instructed. "Watch for the Wolf's Lair sign on the left."

"Got it. Thanks."

Sprinting to her motorcycle, Jassy pulled her sun-streaked blond hair back from her face so she could don her helmet. Then she mounted the bike and started it.

"Hey, Jassy!" Whit called over the noise of the engine.

She glanced back at the grinning old codger. "What?"

"That Seth Heller can be more dangerous than them four-legged critters!" he shouted. "You watch out for The Wolfman!"

Jassy gave him a thumbs-up and spun her BMW cycle out of the gas station. Whit's warning stayed in her mind as she shot down the road, but she wasn't worried. A little risk always made things more interesting. At the Wolf's Lair sign she turned onto a curving road that led upward into a densely forested area. She thrilled at the thought of working with an endangered species; she identified so personally with the fierce independence she associated with wolves.

That the job opening was for a hired *man* didn't daunt her; she was certain she would get the job.

She was going to work with those wolves.

Jassy reached the refuge entrance and dismounted. She wheeled her motorcycle through the gate, leaving it there with her jacket and helmet. On foot, she followed the gravel road uphill to a clearing containing a small wooden building raised on stilts and several fenced-in enclosures surrounded by bleachers. Her pulse beat rapidly as sudden movement in the enclosures caught her eye.

Wolves!

Whit's warning came back to her. A chill ran down her spine and she looked around for another human presence. No one.

Where was he, then—this Wolfman? And what in the world made him so dangerous?

SETH HELLER hadn't thought that finding someone willing to do an honest day's work would be impossible, not with so many jobless people in the area. Luckily he and Ben Lasky, the owner of Wolf's Lair, had gotten the fifty-acre enclosure started before the last hired man had left. A damn shame they'd lost the guy— not that they could really afford to pay a salary, with other expenses rising the way they were. But they had no choice. Most wildlife refuges had local volunteers. Wolf's Lair wouldn't be so lucky.

He walked down the hill from the Laskys' cabin, enjoying the light breeze that fluttered the leaves and carried the sharp, pervasive pine scent that both stimulated and soothed.

Trying to figure out if he could make time to work on the new enclosure that afternoon, Seth was halfway down the sloping road before he paused. Instinct warned him of a stranger's presence. Instinct—and the familiar sounds of twenty-nine restless wolves.

He jogged downhill to the clearing. His heartbeat stopped for a moment. A stranger in a brilliant yellow T-shirt was stooping down in front of the wolf enclosure nearest the small set of bleachers they'd built for visitors, extending an arm to reach through the wire gate. Geronimo and Kaya were closing in fast, the other members of the pack following a short distance behind the alpha male and female.

Seth would trust those wolves with his own life—but not with a stranger's hand.

"Hey, get away from there!" he shouted, running full speed. "What in the hell do you think you're doing?"

The figure straightened immediately and turned. Seth slowed his pace. The stranger was a slightly-built young woman. Her blond hair curled past her shoulders, and moving closer, he noticed her skin had the rich glow of honey. Her clear, vibrant blue eyes were shaded by thick lashes, her lips were wide and full, and her smile was dazzling.

She was like a bright ray of sunshine against the backdrop of the dark, shadowy forest, Seth thought, unwillingly intrigued by this unexpected vision in his territory.

But he was also hot with anger. "Are you crazy, sticking your hand where it doesn't belong? One of those wolves could chew it off before you could blink!"

She seemed startled, but her voice was calm. "I wasn't about to offer myself to some strange wolf for dinner."

"You sure as hell could have fooled me!"

He was still yelling, and she had the audacity to smile.

"I was merely calling the wolves to see if they would come." Her gaze didn't waver; her voice soothed. "I just wanted to see them up close. That's all. Really."

She was either completely innocent or had a lot of guts. Seth intuitively knew it was the latter as she stepped toward him. She smiled. A dimple popped in each cheek, the right one indenting slightly more than the left.

"I'm Jassy Reed," she said, checking him over thoroughly in return. "I'm here looking for work," she went on. "You must be The Wolfman."

Seth scowled. Some of the locals used the nickname to show their contempt, though he had to admit others bestowed the title in a more respectful manner. However she meant it, the blonde seemed amused at his expense, and he didn't like it. He tried to draw on his anger but found it oddly defused.

Jassy was sure she had her man. Seth Heller really did resemble his charges. His thick, dark brown hair and full beard and mustache were streaked with silver, reminding her of the large wolf with dark, silver-tipped fur in one of the enclosures on the other side of the road. This Wolfman had the musculature and presence of a large predator who is certain of his authority, and he moved noiselessly, as well. She hadn't realized he was coming up on her until he'd called out.

Now the area was ringing with the sounds of the wolves calling to their caretaker in whines and sharp howl-barks. They were crowding the fence, jostling each other to get closer to him, some crouching in strange positions. Seth ignored them. His light gray eyes were focused on her intently and she got the uncomfortable feeling he was trying to impose his will on her. But Jassy already knew she should never turn her back on a predator.

Silently they assessed each other.

Jassy lifted her chin, met his eyes squarely and waited.

Finally satisfied, he said, "I'm Seth Heller."

"Yes, I know."

"And I run this place."

"So I was told. I came here looking for you."

"What makes you think you want to work with wolves?"

Jassy figured her answer would determine whether or not he'd consider her for the job. "They're fascinating—"

"I mean, are you a biology student, or just someone who wants to help?" Seth asked.

"I'm not a student."

"Well, that doesn't really matter," he said grudgingly. He crossed his arms over the blue work shirt covering his lean, muscular chest. "Wolf's Lair can always use more volunteers if you're willing to make a commitment."

"Volunteer?" Jassy was disappointed. Economic necessity forced her to find work that paid. "I thought you needed a hired man."

"Wait a minute. Are you telling me you came to apply for the job?" He looked incredulous.

Jassy's hope of being hired was renewed. "That about sums it up."

"Why?"

"Because I need work, of course, and the idea of finding it in a wildlife refuge appeals to me," she answered truthfully.

"Do you always do what appeals to you?"

"When I can. And when I can't, I do whatever I must to pay my own way."

His stare was thoughtful. "You don't live around here."

"Not yet. I have to find a job first," she explained patiently. He finally took notice of the noisy wolves in the enclosure and patted a few heads through the fence.

His back was to her, his attention still on the animals when he asked, "What makes you think you're qualified to be a hired hand?"

If the challenge was meant to put her off, he had another think coming. Jassy was used to people doubting her abilities and wasn't easily dissuaded. Nothing frightened or cowed her—except opening her heart, something very few people had ever required.

She decided the best way to impress the man was with patience and an unflappable attitude. "What makes you think I'm *not* qualified?" she asked good-humoredly. "Don't let my sex or size fool you."

Seth turned around to face her. "I'm not prejudiced because you're female, if that's what you think. I already work with three competent women, but they're volunteers. The hired hand's duties are more taxing and less appealing than what they usually do. I have to expect more of the person who gets this job."

"That's fair enough. I'm not afraid of hard work. I've done things that were taxing before. I worked on a ranch for a while, taking care of livestock and such. I fed them, cleaned up after them. I, uh, got knee-deep into my work."

Seth nodded but gave no sign that he followed her kind of barnyard humor. Maybe the comment had been too subtle.

"So you've worked with animals," he mused. "That's a good start. What about mechanical equipment?"

"I changed oil and greased cars in one of those quickie ten-minute places." When that didn't seem to impress him, she added, "And I know how to do basic repairs on various vehicles. My brother taught me." Along with a few other military men who'd been eager to please an attractive young woman. "I really get a charge out of working on electrical systems."

Jassy couldn't believe that Seth didn't even blink an eye. He just went right on interrogating her.

"Any heavy-lifting experience?"

"I may not be as strong as you are," she admitted, "but I did work on a shipping dock once. That was probably the toughest job I ever had, but not because of the work itself. When the guys realized I was willing to pull my own weight—" she grinned and spread her hands "—they accepted me as one of them."

Seth continued to stare at her thoughtfully. Jassy tried not to squirm, but The Wolfman was a hard nut to crack. He was so serious. So self-contained. He hadn't smiled one at her jokes.

"Sounds as if you move around a lot."

"When I feel like it," she said carefully, sensing he wasn't thrilled by that fact.

"I need a hired man who will be stable."

"I can be stable—"

"For as long as it suits you."

Jassy flushed. True, she moved on when the urge hit her; but so what? A lot of people did. There wasn't a thing wrong with her life-style. She made tons of friends and found exciting new experiences around every curve in the road.

"Are you saying you wouldn't think of hiring someone unless they give you a lifelong commitment?" She joked, "What do you want—a contract signed in blood?"

His lips twitched. Finally. Some proof that he might have a sense of humor lurking beneath that tough hide.

"I'm not quite that demanding."

"Good." Uncomfortable with the idea of fibbing, she decided to be up-front about her intentions. "And to be truthful, I'm looking for a *summer* job. Can you live with that?"

He was silent for a moment, his lips settling back into a straight line. Then he nodded. "I suppose I can settle for a few months. The summer is our busiest period."

"And you obviously haven't found anyone else to take the job," she reminded him.

"Most people are afraid of wolves."

"I'm not. Wild animals fascinate me." Jassy studied the wolves, who had quieted now and sat looking expectantly at Seth. Almost like faithful dogs waiting for a sign of affection. They didn't look so wild. "They're meant to be free, yet they fit naturally into the environment. How nice to know exactly where you belong in the cosmic order of things."

When Jassy turned back to Seth, his expression had changed subtly. His gaze unsettled her, so when he said, "The job doesn't pay much and you'd live in that trailer over at the other end of the enclosures," she took the opportunity to look away.

She spotted the run-down trailer close to the trees. It seemed to sag under the weight of too many years without proper maintenance; but maybe it wouldn't be so bad inside, she told herself. "All I need is shelter from the elements."

"Part of your job will be doing repairs on the buildings and keeping the areas around them mowed. In addition, you'll have to fix plumbing, carry heavy water buckets, remove wolf droppings from the enclosures—"

Jassy smiled. "I'm ready for anything." She thought she had the job, but she wasn't quite sure. Seth obviously wasn't satisfied yet.

He gestured toward the other side of the road, past the central, open area. "We have to finish the new enclosure and there's a lot more fence to put in. You'd have to find time to work on that in addition to your regular duties. Erin and Keith, our summer interns, will help when they're not involved in behavioral studies, and so will I if I can ever find time. It's hard, dirty work."

"No problem."

"So you know how to use a tractor and posthole digger?"

Jassy figured she could forget the job if she said no. She got around the question without really lying. "I worked on fencing at a ranch in Wyoming two years ago." She wasn't about to explain that she'd merely repaired fencing that had already been installed. Before he could probe deeper she asked, "So, do I have the job or what?"

He paused for a heartbeat. "You've got it."

He could sound more enthusiastic. *She* was. Grinning in triumph, she thrust her hand out and Seth shook it. His hand was callused.

"Working outside in the middle of a forest sounds like a great way to spend the summer to me," Jassy went on happily. "What are you going to put in that new enclosure, anyway?"

"What else? A wolf pack. One of the groups that we've tried to keep wild, as separate from human interaction as possible. The larger enclosure will give them fifty acres of relative freedom. It's an intermediary step to letting them out into the wilderness. Want to see what we've done so far?"

"Sure."

At least Seth was enthusiastic about his animals. She walked beside him when he headed down the gravel road. The smaller enclosure was only an acre or so. The wolves had been watching them and followed along the fence as far as they could, then stopped and seemed disappointed at being left behind. That they obviously had a close relationship with Seth touched Jassy. She was prepared to like this man, despite his temper and odd lack of humor.

"I'll be back, guys," Seth promised over their whines. "Those are some of our tame wolves," he explained. "They were hand-raised and so crave human companionship. But don't ever get careless with them. No wolf is ever completely domesticated. You'll have to be properly introduced before you ever step into the enclosure alone. They're always looking for the opportunity to challenge you. Keep that in mind before you get too close."

"I'll remember."

Eyeing Seth, Jassy wondered how much a person would have to know about *him* before getting close. Her new employer was quite a hunk. She'd have to watch her step or she could find herself flirting with the wrong man. The Wolfman was sure to dominate any relationship.

"It's a shame the rest of the wolves can't have fifty acres to roam around in, too," she said. "Even if they are caged, animals should have as much freedom as possible."

"That's what I want for them. As it is, I was lucky to get the grant for one large enclosure. But it's a start. And someday, when people in the area have been educated to view wolves without primitive fear, we'll be able to start setting them free in the wilderness where they belong."

"Do you think they'd know how to keep themselves alive once you released them?"

"A few. Instinct dies hard."

"Only a few? How sad to think you would put so much energy into helping the animals, only to lose them." Glancing back at the wolves, she added, "But I guess they'd have a chance to live the way they were meant to, for however short a time. I think everyone, man and beast, should have that opportunity."

She looked up, surprised to find his expression open. Trusting?

"A Jassy Reed might be just what this place needs," Seth murmured, his mouth curving beneath his mustache.

Jassy blinked in surprise. She'd gotten a natural smile out of him, after all, without even trying. And that was a definite flicker of interest in those unusual gray eyes. Before they'd been cool and challenging; now they expressed warmth and . . . something less definable. An invitation of some sort?

Jassy remembered Whit Bickel's warning. The problem was, she didn't know which side of The Wolfman was more dangerous.

2

SETH ESCORTED JASSY back to the refuge's entrance after showing her the partially completed wolf enclosure. They passed a fairly new, modified A-frame house across the road from where she'd left her motorcycle. Its walls sloped inward to a flat roof rather than the typical peak, and the exterior wasn't quite finished. The grass was too high and the garden was overrun with weeds.

"Your place?" she asked.

"Home, sweet home. As you can see, I'm not much on upkeep. I leave that to the hired man."

If Seth was trying to kid her, he didn't let on. There was an unusual aura about him; a self-contained aloofness that some people might take as unfriendliness. Rather than being put off, though, Jassy felt challenged. She stopped beside the BMW and donned her helmet, keeping the visor raised.

"I had a bike once, when I was a teenager," Seth said, running his hand over the dusty teal-blue fender. "Nothing this fancy, though."

"I bought it last year. I got tired of the work it took to keep the old one running." She swung her leg over the saddle and removed her jacket from where she'd hung it on the dash. Seeing Seth's nostalgic expression as he looked over the machine, she handed the jacket to him and said, "Hop on. I'll save you the walk back."

He didn't need a second invitation.

Once he'd slid in place behind her, Jassy was sorry she'd offered. Seth Heller was a man who affected her in ways she didn't like to admit. She found him wildly attractive, but she'd prefer to keep him at a safe distance so that she had more control.

Doing her best to ignore his muscular thighs pressing against hers and trying not to think about his powerful hands slipping around her waist, she took off fast enough to shake off any uninvited thoughts. And fast enough to make him grab onto her more tightly.

"Whoa, this isn't a dirt track," Seth said, laughing. "And you don't have to beat out any competition."

"Sorry." She adjusted her speed and cruised toward the wolf enclosures. "Will the noise bother the animals?"

"I doubt it. Unfortunately, they're used to just about anything humans can dish out."

"That tame, huh?"

"The hand-raised wolves, anyway. I keep the others and their pups in separate pens. I haven't tried to socialize them in hopes that they'd have a fighting chance if they ever were set free." Seth leaned closer as he spoke. "I've been doing behavior comparison studies of the two main groups in the meantime."

His chest brushed her back with each bump in the road. While he wasn't a really big man—he was as lean as he was muscular—he seemed to envelop her. She edged forward. "So you're a scientist?"

"A field biologist."

Obviously one who knew his subject well. He'd been correct about the wolves' reaction to the motorcycle. Almost nil. A few trotted along the fence and watched as they rode by, while most napped on the flat roofs of their modified A-frame wood shelters that reminded her of Seth's house.

Jassy wished she could as easily ignore the man behind her—a difficult endeavor, considering that she could feel each of his strong fingers splayed over her rib cage. But not for much longer...

She stopped the BMW in front of the trailer that would be hers for the summer and was thankful when Seth quickly dismounted. She could breathe naturally again. She hopped off and removed the roll bag and luggage case from the rear rack, setting both on the ground.

"I can help you with those."

"Thanks, but I wouldn't want you to think I couldn't carry my share of the load around here," she said as she released the saddle bags.

"I wasn't making any assumptions. I just thought you might be anxious to get settled and cleaned up. This isn't a test."

She shrugged. "All right, then."

Seth picked up the last two pieces of gear and led the way to the trailer. When he balanced his load on one hip to open the door, she was riveted by the sight of his neatly encased rear straining against taut jeans. A loud click startled her—the door opening. She looked up and into the interior of her new home, luckily before Seth could catch her staring. Telling herself she had no reason to be embarrassed, Jassy breezed past him and into the living area where she put down the saddlebags.

"The trailer isn't real roomy," Seth said as he followed her in. "But it's big enough for one person."

"At least I'll have some privacy," she said, looking around. "I was renting a room in Cannon Beach."

"So you just came up from Oregon." He placed the luggage case and roll bag next to the others. "Your family live there?"

"No." She didn't intend to talk about anything personal. "I was working at one of the little tourist shops."

He noticed her evasiveness, but all he asked was, "Why did you leave?"

"I was ready to move on."

Jassy wondered if Seth was having second thoughts about having hired her, but he seemed merely curious.

"I'll be working with the wolves this morning," he told her. "I have a few medical problems to take care of."

"You're not a vet as well as a biologist, are you?"

"No, but I couldn't afford to bring one in for routine care. Charlie Metcalf is the local vet. His wife, Fay, who's also his technician, volunteered to be my part-time assistant several years ago. She taught me what Ben wasn't able to." At her puzzled look, he explained, "Ben Lasky and his wife, Ceil, own this land. It's been in Ben's family for generations. He started Wolf's Lair almost thirty years ago."

"Is he a biologist, too?"

"No. Just a bighearted man who took pity on wild animals that were inappropriately kept as pets and domesticated, then turned away when things didn't work out like the owners expected." Seth turned to leave. "Ben's a little gruff, but he grows on you. You'll get to meet him and Ceil later."

"I'll be looking forward to it."

Seth opened the door and paused as if he had something on his mind. All he said was, "Whenever you get settled, come find me. Tie up your hair and wear a long-sleeved shirt so I can introduce you to a few of our wolves. Then I'll show you around the rest of the refuge."

"I won't be long," she promised, closing the door behind him with relief. Despite her considerable people-handling skills, Seth had managed to keep her slightly on edge.

She took stock of her living quarters. The main area was compact but efficient; the walls, furniture and appliances old and a little tacky, but not impossible, she decided. All the place needed was a little brightening up—something she was an expert at. Jassy tried to bring color and cheer to her living environment, wherever that happened to be.

But, first things first.

Unpacking wasn't much of a chore since she traveled light out of necessity. She slipped off her jeans-style leather pants and hung them and her dusty jacket in the narrow hall closet. Though they'd grown comfortable with age and use, she was glad to be rid of the heavier garments she wore for safety. Snow-washed denims and a cotton shirt were more her style.

When she stepped into the shower, Jassy realized the first plumbing she'd have to fix was her own. The water sprayed in fits and starts from the showerhead. And when she tried to adjust the hot water, the handle gave off a screeching sound and the pipes started vibrating. Quickly turning the handle until the noise stopped, she settled for a tepid trickle to rinse off the road dust. Even that felt good. Shampooing hair could wait until later, after she got her hands on some plumbing tools.

Wondering what else needed repair in the trailer, she dried off and quickly slipped into age-softened jeans and a bright blue shirt with long sleeves, as Seth had requested. Then she French-braided her hair.

Now she felt ready for anything—even Seth Heller.

She saw him inside the main enclosure, crouching beside a large gray-brown wolf. He was putting salve on furless patches on the animal's hide. She quietly drew closer and watched.

Seth was patient yet firm with the unhappy-looking wolf. The animals seemed to recognize and respond to his quiet authority. Jassy respected anyone who respected creatures—or people—of lesser capability.

As if some sixth sense had warned him she was near, Seth looked up when she got within a dozen yards. The wolves reacted with noisy agitation.

"That was quick," Seth remarked.

"I told you I wouldn't be gone long. So who is this?"

"Geronimo. He's the alpha male. That means he's the leader of the pack."

Unable to help herself, she asked, "Wasn't that a song? You know—'Leader of the Pack'? Do you think Geronimo would like it if we sang it to him?"

Seth's expression remained perfectly serious when he said, "He'd probably just howl. That song wasn't based on wolves, anyhow. Uh, at least not the four-legged variety."

Jassy raised her eyebrows. Was that Seth's attempt at a joke? She grinned. "I've met plenty of the two-legged kind, but these guys seem more interesting."

"Hey, boy, that's a compliment." Seth patted the wolf hard on his side.

Jassy was amazed when Geronimo nudged him as if seeking more attention, just like a dog.

Seth opened the gate to an adjoining empty enclosure. "I'm going to move most of the pack into this separating pen."

He grabbed one of the wolves by the scruff of the neck and aimed it at the opening. The wolf shot through and three others followed. The animals growled and snapped at each other, making Jassy aware of how dangerous they could be.

Like Seth?

He now urged Geronimo into the other pen, only to have the big male balk and snarl as he grasped Seth's shirtsleeve with his teeth. Seth's reaction was so swift, Jassy stepped back in surprise.

"No, Geronimo." Seth grabbed the wolf's shoulders, kicked his legs out from under him and pushed him flat against the ground. Then he knelt to stare into the animal's eyes. "You don't growl at *me*, buddy."

Seth's tone was stern and commanding. Jassy was amazed that instead of struggling, the creature lay still and whined.

"Had enough?" Obviously satisfied with Geronimo's reaction, Seth let go so the wolf could scramble to his feet and creep through the gate on his belly.

"Dominance ritual," Seth explained, sounding offhand. "Geronimo is very attached to me but his pride requires questioning my authority from time to time."

She felt a bit uneasy. "Uh, do I have to learn to do that? Push wolves down on the ground and tell them who's boss?"

"Not right away. Besides, we'll start you out with the three younger ones. They're easier to handle."

She took a deep breath and told herself she could do anything if she really tried. And Seth wouldn't expect it of her unless the situation was relatively safe.

"The most important thing is to remain centered and confident," he told her. "The animals can sense any weakness."

She nodded. She'd be damned if she'd let either a four-legged or a two-legged creature face her down. As a perpetual new student in numerous grade schools, she'd needed her wits and courage to survive.

As Seth refastened the gate, Jassy noticed that two pens holding smaller wolf packs also adjoined the separating pen. The other setup across the road was similar.

"Are you ready?"

"Ready as I'll ever be."

Her stomach did a queer little dance, a combination of excitement and apprehension at interacting with three wolves. At least a bit of healthy fear would keep her alert, she reasoned.

"Be prepared," Seth cautioned. "These guys are real excited because you're new. They'll jump on you, but they're trained to hook their paws over your arm if you hold it out."

Jassy was squirming just a tiny bit inside as he unlatched the gate. The moment she stepped into the pen, she was surrounded by three whining, wriggling bodies.

"Easy, guys," Seth commanded beside her, using his own body to keep them at bay.

She raised her arm as he'd instructed. In a flash, one of the wolves hooked his paws over her forearm—paws that seemed too large for his long, spindly legs. Then her face was swiped by a large wet tongue. Jassy grinned, making sure her mouth stayed out of the tongue's reach. The wolf's multicolored coat gave him a comical appearance and his amber eyes held a mischievous expression. Jassy started to laugh. With her free hand, she rubbed the wolf's head.

"That's Big Bad," Seth said. "He's the boldest of the juveniles."

Scratching the young wolf, Jassy found a sweet spot on his throat. Big Bad raised his muzzle skyward while he enjoyed the attention. "He's a cutie pie."

"Just remember wolves aren't dogs. They'll keep testing you, so don't get too caught up in their games." He moved behind her. "Hold still. I'm going to tuck your braid away before this smart aleck gets hold of it."

Seth's hands distracted Jassy. His touch felt as gentle as she'd imagined it would. Only more erotic. Not that a pack of wolves could appreciate *that* fact. Seth's fingers were slightly rough and his warm breath along her neck made her tingle with awareness. Her breasts tightened in response. Uncomfortable, she was relieved when Seth straightened the collar of her blouse and moved away. Her renewed concentration came seconds too late.

Big Bad swiped her lips with his tongue.

"Yuck!"

Seth laughed—an amused rumble, low and thrilling. Flustered, Jassy lowered her arm to free Big Bad and greeted the other wolves. Within a few minutes, all three had backed off and relaxed, but didn't take their eyes off her. A fourth pair of eyes—very human and very male—was staring at her with equal intensity.

"You're doing well for an initiate," Seth commented.

Wanting to succeed to impress him and to satisfy herself, Jassy thrilled to the praise.

Seth let the older wolves back onto their home ground one by one. The introductions went smoothly and Jassy felt triumphant when she was even greeted politely by Geronimo himself. A pale cream-and-white wolf lagged behind him.

"Who's the shy one?"

"Her name is Snowbird."

"Come here, Snowbird." Jassy tapped her arm. "Come on. It's all right."

The moment Snowbird grew bold enough to approach, three other wolves rushed in and drove her back toward the wooded part of the pen. Growling and snapping at her, they pinned her to the ground in a more violent-looking version of what Seth had done to Geronimo. Snowbird lay on her side, her legs lifted, her neck arched and vulnerable.

"Hey, what's going on?"

Jassy was about to interfere when Seth stopped her, gripping her upper arm firmly.

She scowled at him. "Aren't you going to stop that?"

Seth shook his head, his watchful gaze on the wolves. "Not unless they get too rough."

Jassy's throat went tight until the fracas ended, seconds later. Thank God no blood had been drawn. She hated violence, whether the perpetrators were human or animals. Amber eyes on her tormentors, Snowbird got up, shook herself off and slunk away toward the far end of the enclosure. The other wolves ignored her.

Seth released Jassy's arm. "I think you've had enough wolf-human interaction for your first day. Let's get out of here." He opened the gate. "Every wolf pack has its hierarchy—like in the military. Snowbird is at the bottom of the heap."

"Yeah, literally."

The joy she'd experienced only a short while before had been obscured by unwelcome memories. "Even wolves have to organize some ridiculous military structure," she remarked bitterly, more to herself than to Seth.

Seth closed and locked the gate behind them. "Sounds like you have something against rules and rituals, Jassy."

"If I do, I'm not alone," she said evasively. Shaking her head in disgust, she headed for the bleachers. "I thought those other wolves were going to tear out Snowbird's throat."

Following closely, Seth assured her, "It wouldn't come to that. The domination/submission ritual rarely does. I *am* worried about Snowbird, though. She was a former pet, but I suspect she didn't get the right treatment from the owners who eventually brought her to Wolf's Lair. She has no sense of self-worth, and this situation isn't helping her any."

"Can't you put her in with a different set of wolves?" Jassy asked as she slid onto the edge of a bleacher.

"I've tried. I was hoping she would find her place here."

Her place . . . What if she couldn't ever find one?

Seth stepped down to the bleacher below and accidentally brushed her arm. Jassy drew away; not to avoid him, but because she was upset and wanted to restore her normal positive mood—something she'd had a great deal of practice at. She just needed a moment to herself.

"I'm hoping the situation is only temporary," Seth was saying as he sat down. "If not, I may have to isolate her."

"Poor Snowbird."

Jassy identified with the wolf. She'd never allowed friendships to go too deep, so she knew what it was like to feel isolated. But, as experience had taught her, she was safer that way. She'd learned to count on nothing and no one except her brother, Dieter. And now she didn't even have him.

Jassy rubbed the tense muscles in her neck. Long ago, she'd learned the power of meditation and techniques of achieving inner tranquillity. She cleared her mind and focused her gaze on the animals, who were settling down for a midmorning snooze. She recalled the images of Big Bad when he'd made her laugh, then when he'd licked her mouth. He really was a cutie pie.

The tension in her neck began to recede as she relaxed. *Nothing's perfect*, she reminded herself pragmatically. When it came right down to it, she wouldn't pass up the opportunity to get to know these animals. They acted out of instinct, not deliberate cruelty. She'd concentrate on appreciating the positive and accepting those things she didn't like. After all, that was the way she got through life. Feeling calmer, she slid off her seat.

"So," she said brightly, "what's next?"

Seth seemed startled by her mood shift, but recovered quickly. "I thought I'd show you around before lunch and explain how the place runs. There are a few odd jobs that need to be done this afternoon. Nothing too taxing."

"How much responsibility will I have with the wolves?"

"Other than cleaning out the enclosures, you'll feed them."

"What do they eat? Canned wolf chow?" Jassy quipped.

Seth *almost* smiled. "No such thing. And I only use veterinary feed when necessary. Since I'm trying to keep

the wolves in the best physical shape, they get carcasses. It's your job to haul them in."

"Carcasses?" Suddenly feeling a bit squeamish, Jassy
wondered if meditating could possibly help her with
this one.

"Some are road kill from the highway. Others are
livestock that died. Either way, we get free feed for the
wolves. Doesn't sound like much, but the money is
sorely needed for other things."

"So I have to pick up dead animals. Great."

Jassy could tell Seth found her discomfort amusing.

"Don't worry." He grinned. "You won't have to pick
up the . . . er . . . feed alone. One of the student interns
will help. As a matter of fact, Keith and Erin brought
in a big buck while you were meeting the pack. And I
saw Ben and Ceil come down from the cabin, probably
to butcher it." Seth rose. "I'll introduce you."

Jassy followed him, her mind in a whirl. Picking up
carcasses that had to be butchered. Oh, boy, what had
she gotten herself into this time?

As they walked along, Seth pointed out the small pen
holding the pups that had been born to the tame packs,
the observation tower built for viewing the enclosures
on both sides of the road, the equipment shed near her
trailer, and, finally, the work/storage building.

Two people were just coming through the doorway,
their voices raised in heated discussion.

"I think we should use household products for the scent rolling tests. Air fresheners, window cleaners, stuff like that," the dark-haired young man stated.

"Oh, right, as if wolves could find those things in the wild." The young woman shook her head, her light brown ponytail bouncing. "I say we should go with natural sources."

"Erin, you can be a pain. We know how they'll react—"

"Whoa!" Seth interrupted. "Rather than argue about it, why don't you each do your own study? But don't go off just yet. Jassy, meet Keith Shapiro and Erin Bennet, two future biologists who couldn't agree on the definition of genetic coding if it killed them. This is Jassy Reed, our new hired man."

"Finally!" Keith said. Behind his glasses, his dark brown eyes swept over her.

Erin smiled warmly. "Boy, are we glad to see you."

Considering they'd probably been taking over the chores, Jassy figured that was true. "Nice to meet you both."

"Now that you're here, we can concentrate on our new study." Keith checked his watch. "It's getting late. Come on, Erin. You can chitchat or whatever girls do later."

"Keith, you're so rude. Don't mind him," Erin called over her shoulder. "He was born with a strange genetic code no one can decipher."

Jassy laughed. "Are they always so compatible?"

"They do have their own style, but believe it or not, when push comes to shove, they work well together. Ben and Ceil must be inside." Seth started toward the door, then stopped and gave her a speculative look. "Wait here. I'll ask them to step out."

"Sure."

Jassy was relieved that Seth had deferred to her uneasiness at watching a deer being butchered. She forgave him his earlier amusement. Remembering the way he'd looked during those few moments, Jassy figured she wouldn't mind seeing him so relaxed again.

A tall, raw-boned man wearing a red-streaked apron followed Seth outside.

"This is our new hired hand?" Ben Lasky didn't seem ready to accept her as easily as the interns had. He inspected her closely. "She's a little thing."

"I'm stronger than I look. Jassy Reed." She held out her hand. Jassy couldn't quite match Ben's grip, but she squeezed hard and refused to flinch.

Ben muttered to himself as if she'd passed the test, then asked, "What kind of a goldurned name is Jassy?"

"It's short for Jasmin," she said. The correct pronunciation bore little resemblance to her nickname.

"*Yazmeen?*" The older man echoed. His eyes narrowed suspiciously. "You a foreigner?"

"Now, Ben, don't give the girl a hard time." A plump woman with salt-and-pepper curls came out of the building. She took Jassy's hand in a no-nonsense shake.

"I'm Ceil, Ben's wife. Don't mind this old geezer. He's always grumping or grouching."

"I was just asking her about her name," Ben insisted.

"I'm one-hundred-percent American. My mother liked the exotic names in Saudi Arabia, where I was born." And had chosen Dieter for Jassy's older brother when the Reeds lived in Germany.

Ben grunted. Seth quickly picked up on her revelation. "Your family was involved with an oil company?"

"No." Jassy reluctantly admitted, "I'm an air-force brat." When Seth stared as if she'd revealed some state secret, Jassy quickly turned to Ben and changed the subject. "So you started Wolf's Lair yourself?"

"You betcha."

"And he'd have you believing he was doing a good job of it by himself, too," Ceil said.

Ben frowned at his wife. "Give me a chance, woman."

Even as she got Ben talking, Jassy knew Seth wouldn't ignore her air-force background. Well, let him dig. He wasn't about to find out anything she wasn't willing to share.

LATE THAT AFTERNOON, Seth drove Jassy to Rudolf's, the local grocery store. Irma Rudolf, the owner, sat at the register and kept an eye on him. She had disliked Seth since he'd once tried to rip off some bread and smoked sausage when he was a kid. He'd been caught, of course, but had refused to admit he was hungry. His widowed mother's poverty wouldn't have been an acceptable excuse.

"Get things for breakfast and dinner," Seth told Jassy. "We usually eat lunch together at Ceil's like we did today. It gives us a chance to talk over our work."

She nodded and sauntered down the second of the store's two aisles. Seth peered over the top of the cereal boxes to watch. Jasmin Reed was something of a mystery.

Why hadn't she told him about her father being in the military when the discussion had come up at the wolf enclosure? She must have spent her whole life moving from one place to another. An air-force brat. Her wandering was starting to make sense, though her reluctance to talk about anything personal was puzzling— and intriguing.

Even more intriguing was her instant rapport with the animals he loved, her trust that they wouldn't hurt her. *Trust.* He wondered if he could trust her. No other "hired man" had ever had the same feeling for the wolves. Any one of them might have taken the idea of picking up carcasses and doing some of the other unpleasant tasks in better stride, perhaps. Not that Jassy had complained. She definitely had guts; that afternoon she'd gone to work cleaning up the wolf enclosures like she'd been doing it all her life.

Selecting some canned goods, he wondered if she approached every job, every move from one place to another, with the same zest. She'd be at Wolf's Lair for only a short time if she stuck to her plan. Would the refuge and its inhabitants—both human and canine—affect Jassy's life as they had his?

"Slow afternoon?" he heard her ask Irma as he was getting a carton of milk from the dairy case.

The storekeeper sniffed. "Most are."

Jassy didn't seem to take Irma's snippy tone as a rebuff.

"It must get pretty lonely when you have to work by yourself," she went on in that warm, cheerful way of hers.

"That's almost always, now that my husband's gone. Can't afford much help but one part-time delivery boy on the weekends. I even have to close up if I want to go out for lunch."

"What a shame. Everyone deserves a break."

"Sometimes I think about closing down. Everybody wants them newfangled twenty-four-hours stores anyhow."

Seth was amazed that Irma had been so open. He'd just learned more about her in the past two minutes than he had in two years. He headed toward the front of the store.

"I even have to lug boxes of goods into the back room myself," she complained. "It's near impossible with my back laid up."

Seth shook his head in wonder. Jassy had a way about her that made people smile, himself included. *A ray of sunshine against a shadowy forest.* She undoubtedly made friends easily; must have them everywhere she'd roamed. He couldn't help being envious of her easy manner, especially when Irma's smile disappeared as he approached the cash register.

"That it?" Irma asked coldly while Jassy moved her bag over to make room for Seth's purchases.

"For today." His curt answer drew Jassy's curious gaze, making him uncomfortable.

Once outside the store, Jassy whispered, "I could tell that woman wasn't thrilled to see us, even though we were paying customers. Does she resent you? Or the wolves?"

"Something like that."

Seth kept his answer vague. He wasn't about to tell her about the shoplifting incident. Besides, that youthful escapade wasn't the only reason Irma Rudolph and most of the townspeople disliked him, and he didn't know Jassy well enough to go into it, either.

Considering the way she'd handled Irma, Seth figured he'd been right when he'd followed his intuition and hired Jassy. She could be good for Wolf's Lair; maybe for him, too. That thought brought with it mixed feelings. While he liked Jassy, was drawn to her, he instinctively knew she might be able to get too close. Still, there was something about her that made him willing to risk an intimacy he'd seldom allowed into his life.

He mulled over his quandary as they loaded the groceries in the back of the pickup truck. Despite Jassy's smiles, her guileless blue eyes, her apparent confidence and inner strength, he sensed turmoil lurking beneath the surface. Why else would she be deliberately evasive about her past?

So they both had things they'd rather keep to themselves. He climbed in behind the wheel. In a way, they were both loners, good at keeping others at bay, even if they did so in ways as different as their life-styles. Seth felt driven to get to know Jassy better and damn the consequences. He waited impatiently until she got settled and adjusted her seat belt.

He hooked an arm over the steering wheel and kept his voice casual. "Listen, Jassy, beating around the bush is not my style. I say what I think . . . and I've been thinking I want to get to know you better."

She turned to face him, her expression startled and wary. "Pardon me?"

"I mean personally." Did he really have to spell it out? "I have a hunch we could have something special together."

Jassy stared, amazed at the statement that had come out of nowhere. They hadn't even been acquainted for twenty-four hours and the man was coming on to her. That had to be a new record in employer-employee relations. *Something special, huh?* Seth Heller undoubtedly wanted to prey on her attraction—her *slight* attraction—to him. Maybe he'd been hanging around wolves too long.

"Uh, I don't think that's a good idea, since I'm working for you," she replied. Her normal confidence had deserted her. Her heart was pounding and her palms were damp. "I'll pass."

She could hardly believe Seth's composure as he shrugged, then started the engine. His expression enigmatic, he simply said, "I think you should reconsider."

He had a nerve. "And what if I don't want to?"

He didn't answer, keeping his eyes on the road as he drove. Jassy tried to relax. Most guys would have come back with another comment, would have kept at her until she got mad enough to tell them off. Either Seth was a cool one or . . . or what?

She glanced his way, but he seemed even more shut off, drawn into himself than usual. Because he wanted to maintain a facade of bravado? Or because she'd hurt his feelings? She couldn't be certain.

Seth was a real mystery. Whit Bickel had warned her about him, and Irma Rudolph had treated him like he had the plague. Why was the town so cold to Seth when he was doing such wonderful work with the wolves?

Despite the fact that she'd just turned him down flat, Jassy's attraction to Seth was increasing by leaps and bounds. She glanced at his profile, his long, silver-tipped dark hair tied back with a strip of leather. He looked a little wild—exciting and scary.

Suddenly she knew what made the man so dangerous. He was the kind of blunt, self-assured man who
could get to her. He was too intense. And getting too
involved with anyone—or any place—was foolish. She
knew that. She just needed to keep her own history in
mind. She wondered if she hadn't gotten in over her
head when she'd linked up with Seth Heller.

Her heart beat even faster. Her reaction was ridiculous. Unwarranted. She had nothing to fear. Once she
got back to her trailer, she'd pull out the travel book she
always carried with her and start figuring out where she
wanted to go when she moved on at the end of the
summer.

3

OPERATING A POSTHOLE digger couldn't be that difficult, Jassy assured herself as she sat aboard the tractor on a steep, rocky slope. She'd worked with all kinds of equipment, and that morning, she'd watched Keith Shapiro closely as he'd dug several postholes. Uneasy with the way the vehicle tilted sideways on the hill, she centered the hydraulic power shaft over the staked area and prayed it wouldn't hit buried rock this time.

"Is everything okay?" Erin called. She was unfastening a big roll of fence wire close by.

"Uh, sure. Fine."

At least, she hoped so. Too bad Keith had taken the afternoon off. This would be one humdinger of a fence, winding up and down wooded hills and skirting boulders and trees.

"I'm glad you're doing that, not me. It looks difficult."

"I'd rather work on flat ground," Jassy admitted, wiping her brow and tying a folded bandana around her forehead. A squirrel chattered in the branches high overhead, and she imagined the rotten little beast was aware of her inexperience. "Oh, chitter, chitter, chitter-shut up or I'll feed you to the wolves!"

Erin laughed. "He would hardly make a mouthful."

"I was joking. I wouldn't want to see such a cute little rodent become a wolf's hors d'oeuvre."

Jassy took a deep breath and grasped the lever. The power shaft droned as it entered the hard ground. When the vibration seemed to slow, she got up on top of the equipment to add her weight. She leaned over and peered at the rotating blades.

"Watch out!"

She jerked upright at the shout.

"Step back!" Seth yelled again as he strode up the hill toward her. "Do you want to get yourself killed?"

"Not particularly." *Great.* He always seemed to be around when she needed to be warned about something. She stepped back onto the tractor and switched the lever to Off.

Coming up beside her, Seth glared upward. "That thing could throw you off. Or worse, you could fall into the blades."

"I guess I wasn't thinking." Though she'd watched Keith stand on the posthole digger all morning, she wasn't about to argue, especially since Seth was so terse. She tried to save face. "Gorgeous day, isn't it?" *Speaking of gorgeous…* She glanced down at the tight white T-shirt that hugged Seth's chest. *Nice pecs, there.* "Anything new and interesting going on with the wolves?"

"No." His eyes remained speculative and distant, his expression suspicious. He rested an arm on the tractor's fender. "Are you sure you know how to run that equipment? I've been watching, and you aren't getting very far."

She shrugged and tried to appear casual. "Okay, I'll speed up. I know the posthole digger is rented."

"Don't rush, for God's sake. Just do the job right."

Uh-oh. He was definitely suspicious. She tried another approach. "Well, hey, everyone has his own way. But if you want to show me how *you* do it, I'm open for some pointers."

"Show you?" His eyebrows rose.

She gestured to the tractor. "Yeah. Climb on, be my guest."

His expression softened, and he climbed aboard so fast, she had to squirm out of the seat and jump off. "I guess it can't hurt to share my personal *technique*."

By the way he said the last word, Jassy knew Seth hadn't been fooled. She moved away as he started the posthole digger, avoiding the pebbles and sod that flew through the air. He didn't seem any more skilled than Keith, though he didn't stand on the power shaft. She'd been using the digger correctly, but inexperience had made her hesitant.

Seth finished the hole and cut the engine. "Ready to take over?"

"Anytime," she said with renewed confidence.

They brushed against each other lightly as she climbed aboard the tractor. Seth's close proximity left her flustered, even after he'd jumped off. She forced herself to concentrate on the work rather than the man who'd shown no further interest in her since she'd turned him down the other day.

Jassy looked around several minutes later, but Seth had disappeared. *Back to work!* She gradually assuaged her guilt over fudging about her experience by working extra hard to make up for her half-truths. She finished a whole row of postholes in an hour. In the open areas between the trees, the blaze of the afternoon sun was particularly hot. Sweat was running down between her breasts, and her mouth was dry. She saw Seth approaching.

He held up a large thermos. "Iced tea. Ceil made it."

"Wonderful!" Jassy killed the tractor engine and jumped to the ground, silently blessing Ben's wife for her thoughtfulness.

Seth filled paper cups for her and Erin. Jassy took hers gratefully, quickly gulping the contents. She helped herself to another, then lay down in the cool shade of a tall maple and propped herself up on her elbows.

Erin flopped down next to her. "Whew, feels good."

"You can say that again."

Seth squatted across from the women. "I think we've done enough fencing for one day." His steady gaze met Jassy's. "You can get back to your chores."

She detected a flicker of personal interest before Seth looked away. "You're the boss," she said.

"You can take one day off every week, you know," Seth told her. "And you don't have to work more than eight or nine hours a day. Just make sure that the chores are taken care of."

She nodded. "Like the wolf buffet. Any carcasses to pick up?" She had yet to carry out her most unpleasant task, but she would find a way to do so when the time came.

"No."

Her relief was short-lived when he added, "But the wolves need to be fed."

She knew there were a couple of unlucky road kills in the refuge's walk-in freezer. She was psyching herself up for the task when Erin brought up a topic that had been worrying Jassy.

"I noticed that the behavior of the other females isn't getting any better toward Snowbird, Dr. Heller," Erin said. "Do you think I ought to check on her?"

Dr. Heller? Seth, who'd indicated he taught university classes from time to time, must have his Ph.D.

He nodded. "We should all keep an eye on the situation."

"Poor Snowbird," said Jassy with feeling. "She just wants to be one of the gang and gets picked on. She's such a pretty animal."

"To you." Erin sipped from her paper cup. "The other wolves aren't impressed. Snowbird doesn't seem to know the subtle logistics of wolf behavior. She doesn't bluff well."

"Bluff?" Jassy echoed.

"An important part of wolf behavior," Seth explained. "Some smaller animals have enough confidence to make themselves dominant."

From the way he was staring at her, he'd undoubtedly realized she could bluff pretty well herself, Jassy thought, amused and a little uncomfortable. "I guess it's like building up armaments, bragging about how many bombs you have or something," she commented. She understood more than she wanted to about military strategy. "You have to outpsyche your enemy."

"That's better than open warfare." Placing his empty cup by the thermos, Seth rose, his thigh muscles flexing and catching Jassy's attention.

She stared as he stood inspecting a pile of fence posts close by. He sure was restless. And usually busy. Jassy wondered if the man ever relaxed. Was he between girlfriends? He didn't seem actively interested in pursuing a woman. At least he hadn't approached *her* again since the other day. She was beginning to question her hasty decision.

"Well, I have to admire anybody or anything that tries to avoid warfare," Jassy continued, trying to keep her mind on the discussion. "I'm a pacifist."

Seth turned. "But wolves are predators, not armies, and their weapons are the teeth and muscles they're born with."

"They have to keep order in the pack," Erin added seriously.

Both women watched as Seth picked up one of the twelve-foot posts and carried it toward the fence line. But Jassy was certain that Erin's respectful gaze was devoid of romantic interest. *No crush on the professor, huh?* Seth was probably thirty-five to Erin's twenty. Jassy was only twenty-six but felt much older. She couldn't remember a time when her father hadn't *expected* her to be mature. Maybe that's why age differences had never stopped her. She'd dated a professor or two in her time.

But Seth Heller wasn't anything like the intellectuals she'd gone out with. He was more a man of the earth. There was something wild, something primitive about his looks and bearing that captivated her. She studied the play of muscles against his T-shirt. They alternately bunched and relaxed as he dragged the post and set it near a hole.

Seth straightened and used the back of a forearm to wipe the sweat from his forehead. The thin T-shirt fabric clung damply to his lean torso. Jassy's mouth went dry, but not from the heat of the day.

Above her, the maple's leaves fluttered in a passing breeze that brought with it the sound of a loud wolf growl from the enclosure below.

Snapping out of her self-induced trance, Jassy glanced over her shoulder. "You know, all this talk of teeth and dominance rituals is getting to me. Don't wolves ever play a game for the fun of it, just to mess around?"

Seth dropped a fence post back on the pile. "Sure, they play. Toss a rubber ball in there, or a scarf or a hat, and watch them go for it. Wolves like to run and play tag and are very affectionate with each other."

"Good. I'd hate to think they were always deadly serious." Like Seth seemed to be for much of the time she'd been around him. Jassy flipped her braid over her shoulder and sat up. "Speaking of fun, *Professor*," she teased, "what do *you* do to wind down?"

"Me?" He seemed amused.

"Do we toss you a rubber ball or something?" Jassy asked.

Erin snickered, then tried to turn the sound into a cough.

"Something soft and round would be nice," Seth agreed.

Jassy caught a wicked gleam lighting up his eyes.

Like a woman?

For a second, her breath caught in her throat as she thought of Seth holding her in those tanned arms. The prospect was, oh, so tempting. And the way he was looking at her right now . . . He'd been keeping himself at a distance the past three days, the way she thought she'd prefer. Still, having fun often involved some degree of risk.

Jassy decided to close the gap he'd kept between them—the gap *she'd* created. She smiled. "Say, isn't there a place where people hang out in these parts? Where you can have a drink with friends, listen to music, have some chow?"

"The White Pine Pub," offered Erin. "Keith and I were talking about going when he gets back tonight."

Jassy locked gazes with Seth. Her heart was pounding much too rapidly when she asked, "Want to join them?" She thought he was going to refuse. "Oh, come on. We'll all have some *fun*."

For the first time in days, he smiled broadly, revealing straight white teeth. "Sure why not?"

What big teeth you have, Jassy mused whimsically, wondering if she should be having second thoughts.

Naw! Surely there'd be safety in numbers.

HOW SOON COULD HE get Jassy completely alone, away from the townspeople who were more strangers than friends? The question had been plaguing Seth from the moment the two of them had settled down at a table in the White Pine Pub. Being around people who had no use for him was something he'd never been comfortable with. Sometimes he thought he was crazy for staying. But how could he ever leave the Laskys or the wolves?

His knee brushed Jassy's and she inched away at the contact. Her denim miniskirt exposed too much leg for a man to ignore. Her hair was loose and tousled and brushed the shoulders of her cream-colored cropped top. Fighting the urge to run his fingers through the silky strands, Seth concentrated on the menu.

"I recommend the steak sandwich and fries, Jassy."

"Give me time to look this over. Figuring out what to order is part of the evening's entertainment."

Seth's gaze was caught by her eyes—mysterious blue pools that glittered in the light from the lone candle on the table. "As you pointed out this afternoon, we could all use some diversion." They probably had different ideas on what that might be. Seth wasn't even sure they were on a date. Perhaps Jassy considered this nothing more than a friendly get-together. She'd made a big deal about meeting the interns and had seemed let down when Keith hadn't come back to Wolf's Lair on time and Erin had used that as an excuse not to join them.

So, was Jassy really attracted to him or what? For once, Seth couldn't tell, for sure—especially not after her previous rejection. Had she finally acquiesced because she decided he was "safe"? Jassy had a surprise coming if she really assumed he didn't know how to howl just because he had a doctorate and taught a university class once in a while. As the high school kid who'd been voted the most likely to end up in prison, he'd had the kind of "fun" back then that she wouldn't care to know about.

But most people in Minal still remembered.

Seth glanced about the huge pine-paneled room, noting an old man glaring at him from the bar. The couple at the next table had looked right through him as if he didn't exist, as had the guys playing pool in the alcove opposite the empty dance floor. He was glad they'd made it in early so the place wasn't packed. Maybe Jassy wouldn't have a chance to notice how the locals felt about him.

"I think I'll stick with a hamburger," she said decisively.

"That's up to you, but even if it's a good one, a burger is a burger."

"True, but I haven't had that many in my life." When he gave her a disbelieving look, Jassy said, "I've only been eating them for a few years."

"You didn't have hamburgers when you were growing up?"

She shook her head. "My father was stationed in various foreign countries and he always insisted we eat local cuisine."

Another interesting piece of history to store away. She didn't give out many, that was for sure.

The waitress stopped at their table and took their orders. Across the room, the bartender, a woman Seth knew, caught his eye and winked at him. The first friendly gesture he'd received since entering the place. He nodded and waved. He'd had a little fling with Maggie when she'd been between husbands a few years back. She'd never held anything against him but her lush body.

He turned to Jassy. He wanted to know her better. "You're so interested in animals. Did you study biology or zoology in school?"

"Nope." Jassy tossed back a strand of her hair. "The universities I attended didn't have courses dealing with animals that appealed to me. But I did study marine biology...."

"Universities?" Another revealing detail. "How many did you attend?"

"Oh, several."

"What does that mean? Three or four?"

"That means *several*," she said emphatically. Paying no attention to his startled reaction, she went on quickly, "Marine biology was one of my favorite classes. We even went diving on coral reefs to observe tropical fish in their natural environment. You should have seen the colors...."

"If marine biology is so fascinating, how come you didn't get a degree in the subject?" he interrupted, goading her.

"How do you know I didn't?"

"Anyone who skips from school to school could never get enough credits together. I'd be willing to bet you don't have a degree of any kind."

Her annoyance was quickly hidden by a smile. "Okay, so I don't have a degree. Not that real knowledge can be measured with a piece of paper. And not that I thought I needed an education of any special sort to do the job at Wolf's Lair."

Hmm, the lady was getting prickly. He decided to back off. "Really? You mean you didn't prepare a professional résumé for our interview?" he joked. At least he knew he could drag information out of her when he wanted to. He'd wait for something more important before he did so again. He smiled. "I thought you just forgot to give it to me."

She relaxed at his teasing. "I promise it'll be on your desk tomorrow."

"I don't have a desk. Nail it to a fence post."

"I'd rather snag it on one of Geronimo's fangs and let him keep it for you."

They both laughed.

"I wasn't trying to give you a hard time," Seth said. "You're very intelligent and obviously have the potential to do whatever you want."

"I *am* doing what I want," she insisted.

A little too strongly, he thought. All right. The subject was definitely closed. Obviously Jassy was defensive about her life-style.

The beer arrived. Maggie delivered the tall glasses herself, sidling close to Seth and brushing her hip against his arm.

"How are you doing?" she asked softly.

"Not bad. You? I heard you were getting married again."

"Oh, yeah. One of these days."

She was very casual about her fiancé from the way she was flirting with him, Seth mused. But Maggie had always been a wild woman—the type he used to run around with in his younger years. He still liked her. She didn't put all kinds of qualifications on friendship.

Maggie batted her lashes. "I haven't seen you in months. You must be awfully busy with those wolves."

"I have plenty to do." He usually avoided places where he wasn't welcome. Maggie was the exception to the rule.

"Well, you ought to drop by when you get a chance," Maggie told him throatily. "I'll give you a free...drink." She smiled before walking away, hips swinging.

Seth realized Jassy had watched the whole interchange with amazement. If her brows arched any higher, they would disappear into her hairline. Amused, he took a swig of beer.

"This sure is gorgeous country," Jassy said, looking for a safe topic. She leaned forward and placed her elbows on the table. "When I get a chance, I want to take a long trip into the mountains and camp out. That's the only way you get a real feel for a wilderness area."

"I've always been into camping," Seth told her. If she would consider going with him, that would be one way to get her completely alone.

Jassy gave him a big grin that made him feel a little less alone. "There's nothing like looking up at a sky full of stars at night, is there?"

"It's romantic, all right."

"Nothing like fresh air and lots of exercise," she added, looking away.

Seth could tell she'd followed his train of thought— and then was neatly deflecting it. She was like a butterfly that flitted away whenever one came too close. What was she afraid of? Before he could find out, or test further the quickness of her response, the food arrived. They got serious about appeasing their empty stomachs by keeping conversation to a minimum.

Seth was working on the second half of his steak sandwich when two plaid-shirted men entered the establishment. He knew the shorter, barrel-chested one. Bull O'Hara was a chronic ne'er-do-well and petty criminal, a onetime rival of Seth's in high school. A dropout, Bull had never made it to college and now worked at odd jobs and had a reputation for drinking and brawling. The two men moved to the far end of the bar where they joined the old guy who'd been glaring at him earlier.

They'd finished their sandwiches and had each ordered a second beer when Jassy said, "That jukebox is neat, a real collector's item. I could use some more upbeat music, though. I've heard enough country. I wonder if there's any rock."

"We can go look," Seth offered, rising to pull out her chair. They both headed for the machine.

As Jassy examined the selections, he admired the sheen of her pale hair in the dim light. "Do they have 'Leader of the Pack'?" he asked.

She chuckled. "Hmm. Lots of oldies, but I don't see it. How about this one?"

She was pointing to "The House of the Rising Sun" by a group called The Animals. Giving her a wily grin at what he was sure was her idea of a subtle joke, Seth put in some coins. She punched the number of the sexy old rock tune, then chose several others, among them "Wild Thing" by the Trogs. Seth wasn't about to pass up this opportunity.

"Let's dance," he said, taking her hand and whirling her into his arms as the first strains of music filled the pub.

She blinked in surprise. "Uh, sure."

Not that he really gave her a choice. He was already leading her onto the open space that served as the dance floor.

Seth cradled Jassy against him, knowing just where to fit her hips, how close to nestle her breasts so her nipples brushed lightly against his chest as they moved to the slow, throbbing beat. She raised her arms and hooked her hands around his neck. Her cropped top pulled up, exposing her midriff; he slid his palm over warm, bare skin. A single touch and he was aroused. He breathed in her light fragrance and rubbed his cheek against her satiny hair.

Several other couples joined them on the floor. Seth paid no attention to them. Rolling his hips to the rhythm, he pressed the small of Jassy's back, his knee grazing her inner thighs as he led her in a turn.

She made a quiet noise, then cleared her throat. "Um, maybe we'd better go back to the table." Her voice was husky, and a little shaky. "We can dance after we have dessert."

Unwilling to interrupt the delicious contact, he ignored her ploy and kept dancing. This was *his* dessert, and he wasn't about to let her run away from their mutual attraction as she seemed so fond of doing. Jassy might not be as easy to read as other women, but, unless he'd completely lost his ability to recognize male-female chemistry, she was enjoying the close contact every bit as much as he was. Her fingers dug into his neck, the sharp pressure more provocative than a gentler touch.

Jassy felt so right in his arms.

When he turned her again, they made full contact. He could tell she was aware of his state of arousal. This time, instead of trying to come up with some silly excuse to get off the dance floor, she clung to him even more tightly.

And when the music changed, he only paused for a heartbeat until a faster number started to play—"Born to Be Wild", by Steppenwolf. Jassy's sense of humor wouldn't give him a rest.

He whirled Jassy out away from him, then drew her back close, pressing her body against his from chest to knee. Their gazes met and they spoke without words. If this evening hadn't started out as a date, he was determined it would end like one. Savoring the feel of the smooth warm skin at her waist and midriff, he used his hips and his hands to guide her through the fast-paced steps.

Jassy felt a bit breathless. She was grateful the up-tempo song was giving her the respite she needed from continuous close contact. She leaned her head back to look Seth full in the face.

"Whew! Did you take a course in ballroom dancing?"

He slowed a bit. "No, but I've had plenty of experience in barroom dancing."

"You used to hang out in bars?"

"I didn't learn my technique at the senior prom," he assured her. "Though I did enjoy that occasion . . . from the parking lot . . . in the back seat of a car."

Jassy felt her face warm at what her imagination conjured up with that information. She hoped Seth would assume her coloring was from exertion, but his slow, laid-back grin told her otherwise. He pulled her close again, moving with a natural grace that was easy to follow. While he picked up the pace of the music, he didn't loosen his hold on her.

If he kissed her now, right in the middle of the dance floor, she wouldn't be able to resist.

His breath lightly feathered her temple and sent a ripple of desire coursing through her. She shifted restlessly in his arms, savored the feel of his cotton shirt under her palms. She breathed deeply, sighed as she caught the scent of his after-shave. One of Seth's hands rested right below her breast, and she was achingly, uncomfortably aware of its position. He would only have to slide his fingers up an inch or so, and . . .

Pulse pounding in her throat, Jassy sought escape. Luckily the last strains of the piece were just dying off. She pulled free.

"Whew! I'm warm—too much beer." Ignoring Seth's challenging expression, she quickly said, "I'll just take a short trip to the ladies' room and splash some cold water on my face."

"Why don't we take a walk outside instead?"

Alone together beneath the stars? Her pulse raced. Trying not to seem too obvious, Jassy backed away before he could make any sudden move to reclaim her.

"The ladies' room is a better idea. I'll see you in a minute."

She whirled and made her getaway. She'd never before used a ladies' room as a sanctuary, but she could suddenly see its merit as a place to relax. To take several deep breaths. To get annoyed with herself.

Seth wasn't the first man who'd ever turned her on. *So why was she so uptight?* Jassy wondered as she splashed cold water on her face. The man's intensity frightened her. His knowing stare seemed capable of stripping her naked—and not just physically. If she wasn't careful, he would seduce all her private thoughts from her. She should keep him at a distance; but she wasn't sure she wanted to .

What a predicament!

Drying her face and hands with a paper towel, she peered out the ladies'-room door before she went back into the restaurant. Seth had returned to their table. Good. She could use a little perspective before she got too close to him again.

Determined to get her mind on something other than The Wolfman, Jassy paused at the alcove where several men were standing around, watching a game of pool. One of the men had a difficult shot.

A short, burly man in a plaid shirt and billed cap grinned at her. "Get bored with your boyfriend?" He weaved closer. "Looking for some'un else?"

She noted the boilermaker in the guy's hand. No wonder he couldn't walk or talk straight. "I'm not bored. I wanted to see how the game was going."

"Watch this shot." The skinny man with the pool cue leaned across the table and showed off for her, easily making the combination.

"Not bad." Jassy smiled and was about to walk away when the stocky man stepped in front of her. His breath reeked of booze.

"What're you doing with that bozo from the wolf zoo, anyhow?"

Though she'd realized Seth wasn't the most popular man in town, she wasn't prepared for this kind of hostility. "I work at Wolf's Lair."

"You a scientist or something?"

"Just a handyman—er, person." The guy was making her nervous, but Jassy saw no reason to be rude. "I build fences, clean up, stuff like that."

"Buildin' a fence? Gonna put them damned wolves in a big pen where you can't even keep track of 'em?" His bloodshot eyes narrowed and he pointed an accusing finger at her. "Well, they're gonna get out and then we'll have to shoot 'em."

He was definitely an unpleasant fellow. "They aren't going to get out, and you shouldn't even think about shooting an endangered species."

Another man, a tall redhead, crowded her. "I'd say wolves were a *dangerous* species, wouldn't you, Bull? Give 'em a chance and they'll come down on this town and rip out our throats."

Jassy wanted nothing more than to get back to her table and more congenial company, but couldn't help trying to reason with the men first. She repeated something that Erin had told her: "There's no recorded incident of a healthy wolf attacking a human in the United States, you know. Wolves don't consider humans prey."

"Yeah?" the redhead challenged. "Maybe the victims didn't live to tell their stories."

"I'd shoot every one of them critters if I could," Bull added. Setting his glass down on the edge of the pool table, he mimed holding a rifle. "I'd pick 'em off, one by one. Pow!"

There was no reasoning with this guy. "How brave," Jassy muttered as she tried to step around him.

Bull stuck out his arm, grabbed the side of the pool table and effectively blocked her path. "You insulting my manhood?"

"That was an insult if I ever heard one," the redhead said, drawing closer.

Alarmed, Jassy held out her hands and immediately retreated. She'd said the wrong things to the wrong people. "Hey, I'm sorry, I didn't mean to insult anyone." She gestured to the table. "I just wanted to watch some pool. We're holding up the game. How about letting me buy all of you a round of beer?"

"Sounds good," said one of the players.

But Bull glowered and stepped closer, cornering her. "Don't try to get out of it. You insulted me on purpose. I don't like women with big mouths, no matter how pretty they are."

"I said I was sorry." Jassy tried to go around Bull the other way. The redhead was blocking her. Her throat tightened. She forced a smile to her lips and bluffed, "Excuse me, but I have to get back to my friends."

"You ain't goin' nowhere."

Bull reached out with a ham-size hand and shoved her squarely in the chest. Jassy went flying back against the pool table and whomped her shoulder on its edge as she fell. Angry, trying to keep her wits about her and to figure out what to do next, she slowly rose.

"Keep your hands off the woman!"

Startled, she looked toward the other end of the pool table. Seth had arrived.

Bull turned his back on Jassy. "You threatening me, Heller?"

Seth seemed calm and deadly serious. "Call it what you like, but don't touch her again."

Bull reached into his pants pocket. "You think you're really something, don't you, Wolfman? I think you've been hanging around with them critters too long." He pulled something out.

With a snap of his wrist and a loud click Bull's switchblade locked into place.

4

JASSY FROZE as Bull brandished the knife in Seth's face.

"Ha-ha! Like this kinda claw, Wolfman?" Bull sneered.

Even drunk, the stocky man was fully capable of inflicting serious injury. To divert Bull's attention, Jassy exclaimed, "Hold on here!"

But Seth was already making a lightning-swift move. Grabbing Bull's knife hand, Seth hit him with a body slam from the side. Knocked off balance, Bull fell backward and landed on the floor with a thud.

"Oof."

The knife skittered away.

Seth quickly picked up the weapon and pinned Bull down with a knee across his legs and a hand in the middle of his barrel chest.

"Chill out," Seth commanded, staring into his adversary's eyes. "You're drunk."

Jassy recognized Seth's manner. He was handling Bull the same way he had Geronimo—with quiet authority.

"Damn it!" Bull muttered, unsuccessfully trying to get up.

Seth leaned on him harder and grabbed his throat. "I said, *chill out*."

"Hey, what the hell!" complained Bull's redheaded buddy. He pushed past a couple of the other pool players, all of whom had been watching the fracas.

Jassy stepped right into his path to block him.

"Hey!" he growled at her, placing his hands on her shoulders to push her aside.

But she bent her knees and braced herself, finding the rock-steady "center" she'd learned practicing martial arts. If she had to, she'd flip him—a move that would stall him, perhaps even hurt him. Unfortunately, Bull seemed to have more than one pal.

"What's going on?" a big bruiser asked, approaching from the bar. Several of the other pool players also crowded menacingly toward Seth.

Jassy was afraid there was going to be a free-for-all. Still keeping Bull pinned, Seth remained cool, his steady gaze flicking from the fallen man to the menacing crowd that was gathering. Although he wasn't holding the knife in a threatening fashion, Jassy got the distinct impression from the way he crouched that Seth knew how to use it. Beneath him, Bull drunkenly mouthed obscenities.

Seth turned back to him. "I mean it, Bull, simmer down!" His expression was fierce, his teeth bared. "Don't be pulling knives on people . . . unless you want your neck broken!"

This time Bull quieted. And the crowd drew back when Seth rose to face them. He was up against a dozen men, but he showed no fear, Jassy noted. His scowl was a warning for anyone who thought to attack him. Keeping his eyes on the surrounding men, Seth threw the knife onto the pool table, out of Bull's reach, and motioned to Jassy. "Come on."

He walked behind her and guided her back to their table. The crowd parted to let them through. Jassy glanced over her shoulder and saw the redhead helping Bull to his feet. Neither of the men made any effort to come after Seth. They'd obviously been as cowed by The Wolfman's icy courage as the rest of the locals.

Jassy was also impressed. She knew few men who would have been willing to face down one bully for her, much less a bunch of them. Not that she would have expected—or wanted—anyone to put himself on the line for her like that. She'd always managed to take care of herself in tight situations, and she didn't need to be "rescued."

She was about to tell Seth that when he threw some money on the table for their dinner, grabbed her denim jacket and headed for the exit without waiting to see if she followed. And yet, obviously confident that she would, he held the door open for her.

"Thanks," Jassy remarked dryly as she passed him. "You're a regular hero, aren't you?"

He took her arm and led her down the steps and across the gravel parking lot toward his pickup truck.

Jassy grew more and more uncomfortable with his tense silence. When he unlocked the door for her, she was quick to open it and climb in. Circling the vehicle, Seth jumped in the other side and started the engine.

After turning out onto the highway, he asked, "Now, what was that crack about a hero?"

Despite the jerky ride, she managed to slip on her jacket. "Oh, nothing."

Jassy was ashamed that she'd been a little turned on by Seth's protectiveness. A believer in nonviolence, she didn't *want* to be thrilled when a man threatened to break someone else's neck to keep her safe. Glancing out the window, she tried to push her discomfort aside by focusing on the silhouettes of the evergreens they passed along the roadway.

A few minutes later, her emotions under better control, Jassy decided to be up-front with Seth.

"I could have taken care of myself back there, you know. I've talked my way out of rough circumstances more than once in bars and on air-force bases."

"You've been up against jailbirds before?"

"That Bull guy has served time?"

"He's in and out of the county jail at least once or twice a year," Seth told her.

"For what?"

"Theft, assault—you name it. He was arrested for slicing up a guy in a knife fight a few months back. I believe he's still on probation."

Jassy swallowed hard, relieved that Seth had been around, after all. Still, she felt compelled to continue her challenge on principle.

"But the man didn't pull his knife until you came on the scene. And I don't think you needed to threaten him like you did."

"That was talk," Seth said tersely. "Unfortunately, the only kind men like Bull O'Hara understand."

"You wouldn't really break anyone's neck?"

"Not unless I had to."

Wondering if Seth was just trying to appear macho, Jassy tried to deflate his ego a little. "I know some martial-arts moves that could have stopped Bull without hurting him at all."

"Really? Did you have a class in judo at one of those universities?"

His response was mildly inquisitive—not at all the reaction she'd expected. He wasn't buying into her argument.

"When I was a teenager," she informed him, "my brother and I studied various disciplines in Japan."

"So you do admit to having family members somewhere on earth," Seth noted. "Where does your brother live now?"

Jassy's jaw tightened. "Nowhere. He's dead." She felt Seth's gaze on her. "Dieter was one of the marines who was killed in the Persian Gulf a few years back."

Seth's reaction was quick and sincere. "I'm sorry." He glanced at Jassy; she was staring straight ahead into the darkness. No wonder she was preachy about war and violence, he thought.

Knowing he was pushing it, he probed, "Were the two of you close?"

"Since Dieter was my only sibling, I would say so."

Seth sensed Jassy was trying to hide the true depth of her feelings. He cared deeply about his own two sisters, although he rarely had contact with them anymore. "His loss must have been devastating. What about your parents?"

"They're both alive," she said, sounding resigned to giving him some information to keep him satisfied. "My mother lives in Ohio. I could care less where my father is stationed. The colonel and I never got along, and now that he and Mom are divorced, I don't have to see him anymore." She took a deep breath. "Now, let's get off this topic, okay?"

"All right." *For now, at any rate.* Seth could tell she was upset.

Jassy remained silent as he turned off the highway and drove up the winding road that led to the refuge. The dense foliage nearly blotted out the light from the full moon overhead.

When they'd entered the gates, she told him, "You can let me off by the trailer."

He didn't intend to let her go that easily. He shot right past it. "I'm going to park the truck by the equipment shed. Then I'll walk you back to your trailer."

She sighed, vexed. "That's not necessary. Surely it's safe enough out here. And I already told you I'm capable of taking care of myself."

Seth wasn't concerned for her safety at the moment, but he wasn't about to tell her that he wanted her company. They'd started to establish a real rapport, yet she seemed set on pulling away.

"You don't have to keep telling me how tough you are, Jassy. I know you have to be gutsy to travel around the country alone on a motorcycle." He pulled up beside the shed and switched off the ignition. "And I've already seen your courage dealing with the wolves."

"Then what's the big deal about walking me to my trailer?" she asked, reaching for the door handle.

Seth's hand stopped hers. "I want to talk." *And keep you near me.*

"We've talked enough."

"About *you* maybe. But I need to tell you a few things about me and my relationship with the town before you go back there," he said, releasing her hand. "You didn't really know what you were getting into tonight."

She shifted uncomfortably but didn't try to leave. "Surely the townspeople don't hate wolves enough to beat up the Lair's staff."

"Some people hate *me* more than the wolves. You were waving a red flag in front of their faces when you walked into the White Pine with me."

Seth leaned back and wedged his shoulder against his door to give her some breathing space. Jassy turned toward him, but he couldn't see her expression in the dark.

"I was Minal's number-one hellion as a kid," he continued. "I got into a lot of trouble." Seth didn't intend to spill his guts, but the situation had been his fault as much as hers, and she needed to know that.

"What kind of trouble?"

"Vandalism, shoplifting . . . other things."

Including more serious thefts by the time he was fifteen; he'd once been caught selling stolen booze behind the high school auditorium. And then there'd been the fights, most of which he'd won. Unfortunately, several of his adversaries had had parents willing to be tattled to. And the parents had gotten the law on him.

"People are still holding your past against you?" Jassy asked, incredulous. "But surely they wouldn't have been on Bull's side tonight. He's no angel."

"Most upstanding citizens steer clear of him, though they may share his attitude toward me and the refuge." *Small-minded and unforgiving as the self-righteous are,* he silently added. "People don't want to mess with Bull and his pals. No one would have come to our aid if there'd been a real fight."

"They wouldn't even have called the police?"

Seth shrugged. "Maybe. But I wouldn't bet on it. I hope you'll be more careful about who you turn your charms on in the future. For your sake."

He'd expected her to bristle at that, but she said, "You mean Bull O'Hara."

"Him especially. We were big rivals in high school until I straightened up my act and started working for decent grades. About the same time, he flunked out."

"Maybe he resents your success."

"I'm not rolling in money."

"Money isn't everything. You went from juvenile delinquency to higher education and a professional career."

Seth laughed. "Bull and his sort don't care about education or careers. More likely he was jealous that I had a pretty companion tonight."

Jassy was quiet for a moment. "The decent townspeople should respect your achievements," she said finally, "even if they don't like your wolves."

"A few might. The rest probably think I have my nose in the air." *And continue to call me "white trash" behind my back.* Seth had no more use for those people than they had for him, but he wasn't about to get into that. "Just be more cautious in future," he reiterated.

"All right," she agreed. "I consider myself warned."

Seth wasn't sure she would take that warning to heart. Or *could* take it seriously. Jassy was a very outgoing woman, and, despite being on her own in the world, she was a bit too trusting, in his opinion.

She was gazing out the window. Crickets chirped riotously and a cool breeze carried the crisp smell of pine needles and the unmistakable aroma of damp earth. As usual on the Northwest Coast, rain had fallen recently somewhere nearby.

Seth thought about the way Jassy had pressed herself against him when they'd danced. He was tempted to reach for her now. The thought of her warm body against his was very inviting.

"It's getting late," Jassy announced, interrupting his musing. "I guess I should be going to bed."

Bed. Her remark and his unspoken desire played havoc with Seth's imagination. Holding Jassy naked, skin against skin— But he was jumping ahead of the game.

When she climbed out of the pickup, he joined her on the gravel road that wound between shadows and the glow of the all-night security lights. At first they didn't speak as they strolled toward the trailer, which was fine with Seth. He often preferred companionable silence to conversation. The wolves in the nearest enclosures remained quiet, though subtle movement made him aware that the animals were watching him.

Jassy turned onto the path that led to the trailer. "You know, a creep like Bull O'Hara shouldn't be the only one who can find friends in Minal."

Seth couldn't believe her mind was still on the incident at the White Pine Pub. "Bull's welcome to the lowlives who usually hang out with him. I don't want them."

"But you could probably find a better class of people to associate with if you tried. I can't believe every single person in this area is of the same mind-set. Or is completely unwilling to change."

Jassy slowed her pace. She was making Seth edgy. She had to be diplomatic if she wanted to get through to him.

"Sometimes a little extra friendliness goes a long way," she continued. "Kill them with kindness, if you know what I mean."

"Instead of threatening to kill people physically?" His gaze was fixed resolutely on the path.

"Have you ever thought about trying to educate people? Maybe offer some free lectures on wolves and the environment and endangered species at the local library? That would show the town a different side of you."

"I'm sure the library would be tickled pink."

She ignored his sarcasm. "I'll bet the library would love it! You could recommend books for adults and kids. And speaking of kids," she went on, her enthusiasm growing," how about taking a wolf pup to school for a science class?"

"Ceil has visited the school with pups a few times."

"But if you appeared in person, you could also give a spiel about improving oneself and getting an education. Surely the parents would like that, don't you think?"

He gave her a sidelong glance and grunted.

Jassy refused to be discouraged. "If you shared some of your personal background, you might even help a few kids clean up their own act. That would certainly be a boon to the community."

"I'm not sharing my background," he snapped irritably.

"Well, okay," she relented. "You don't have to go that far. It was only a suggestion. Giving talks at the library or the school would be good enough PR."

"Or good B.S."

She stopped a few yards from the trailer. "You think that publicity is B.S.?"

"If it's meant to impress Minal with my worth, yes. I am what I am. People can take me on my own terms or go to hell, for all I care."

Great. She was trying to reform his attitude and she'd managed to antagonize him instead.

Disappointed that he wasn't in the least bit open to her ideas, she groused, "What a fine attitude."

"I'm not a Goody Two-Shoes."

"Meaning *I* am?" She was annoyed at his barb.

He gazed at her steadily, his eyes unreadable.

"Trouble can't be pushed aside with a few cutesy smiles."

"Cutesy?" Jassy frowned. "You don't know anything, Seth Heller. If a real smile ever crossed your lips, your face would probably crack."

Jassy refused to let Seth's fierce expression frighten her. Though no longer an angry, mixed-up child, he obviously couldn't forget his experiences. Otherwise he'd try to meet his neighbors halfway—just sparing a few minutes for small talk. He'd been incredibly cold toward Irma Rudolph the other day, and he hadn't approached anyone at the White Pine Pub until he'd challenged Bull. But she wasn't about to mention anything that he could take as criticism.

"At least I'm honest," Seth announced.

She snapped to attention. "What? Now you're saying I'm not honest?"

"You may smile a lot but you're not as happy as you try to make out."

"You don't know that!"

"Anybody with half a brain and a little patience can see right through you."

"Anybody as crafty and paranoid as you might think that." She'd admit to her deepest feelings only when *she* decided to. No one had the right to invade her emotional space. "You'd do better to use your incredible powers of observation on the townspeople," she insisted, turning the spotlight right back on him. "They can't be as bad as you think."

"I'm not interested in the townspeople. I'm interested in you." He stepped closer, looming over her. "Not that you seem to appreciate that. Or else you're afraid. We could have had a real date tonight."

His remark about fear added to the tension of their argument and made her reckless. "I thought we *were* on a date." That certainly silenced him, she noted with satisfaction. She could handle him. Feeling cocky, she added, "But you sure have a crummy way of saying good-night."

"I haven't said good-night at all," Seth muttered drawing her against him so quickly and tightly that her breath caught in her throat. Jassy expected him to kiss her when he lowered his head. Instead, he ran his fingers through her hair and buried his face in the long curls as if memorizing their scent. She shivered as his warm breath feathered her throat and ear.

Finally, he slanted his mouth over hers. The kiss started slow and soft. His beard felt silky, his lips smooth. Jassy's heart flip-flopped when his tongue caressed her mouth, then invaded.

Suddenly feeling helpless, she realized she couldn't handle The Wolfman, after all.

He had one hand splayed across her upper back and he cupped her hip with the other. He pressed their bodies into full contact and Jassy's breasts flattened against the firm wall of his chest as her arms slid up to circle his neck. She could feel the proof of his arousal against her belly. Whether she wanted to or not, she desired him— with a wild, almost painful longing. Instinctively she undulated her hips, realizing she was doing so only when he began to move his hips against hers.

He slipped a hand under her jacket and top, skimming her back, running his fingers down her spine. She shivered at the delicious contact.

He seemed to know exactly where to touch her, just as he seemed to sense her deepest feelings. The very idea was frightening—and arousing. Jassy was torn. She should end this, but she couldn't bear to make Seth stop kissing her. She moaned when he broke contact to lave her cheek and ear.

"You taste so good," he murmured against her mouth, then kissed her deeply.

His hand found its way to her breast where he stroked a nipple through the lace of her soft bra. Then he slipped his fingers beneath the fabric and pulled the garment up. Her breasts seemed to swell into his callused palms, with a dizzingly sensual effect. Secret dreams becoming reality, she thought.

But this *was* reality, Jassy realized with ever-increasing awareness. They were going much too far, much too fast.

"Um, wait." She managed to place her trembling hands against his chest and put a couple of inches between them.

He stared down at her, his breath uneven, and stroked her breast lazily.

"Wait just a minute," she said more loudly. She took hold of his hand to move it down and away from her breast. "Let's, um . . . save this for another time, shall we?"

"Shall we?" His pale gray eyes didn't waver.

Seth held her hips against him, her miniskirt pulled up to the tops of her thighs. The hand she'd pushed away from her breast now slid up her leg. Jassy reacted quickly, catching his hand before he encountered her lace-edged panties. Seth hadn't been kidding when he'd said he was a fast one with the ladies.

"Let's *definitely* save this for another time," she insisted, pulling at her skirt while pushing harder at his chest.

She nearly stumbled when he suddenly released her. Shakily, she backed up a few steps.

"So when's the next time to be?" he demanded.

"When's our next *date*, you mean?" She was not planning to go to bed with him and she was going to be up-front about it.

"How about tomorrow night?"

All of a sudden, she wasn't even sure she wanted a date. Maybe she could put him off. "Um, let's make it Saturday."

He frowned. "That's a long way away."

Right. Time enough so they would both cool down. "I have a lot of work to do," she pointed out.

"I'll give you time off."

"No, no. Saturday will be fine. I've decided Sunday's going to be my day off. You said it was my choice."

He nodded. "All right, Saturday."

"We could go to a movie or something, couldn't we?" At least some structured plans would make her feel more relaxed when she was with him.

"We could go over to Pineville," he said. Jassy had heard of the town, about ten miles from Minal. Seth grinned, his teeth white in the moonlight. "Pineville has a drive-in."

Jassy's knees grew weak at the very thought. "I prefer regular movies myself."

Seth gazed at her. "Really? Any particular reason?"

He could probably make a very good guess. Feeling her face grow warm, she hedged, "I hate those tinny sound boxes they have at drive-ins."

"I think there's also a movie house in Pineville."

"Sounds fine." She retreated another couple of feet until her back rested against the trailer. Keeping her voice light and cheery, she said, "Boy, I'm tired. I'm going to go in now. I need my sleep so I can do a good day's work. See you tomorrow."

Chuckling, he murmured, "See you," and slipped off into the darkness.

Jassy leaned against the trailer until her heartbeat slowed to normal. She glanced up at the sky—a black sea awash with thousands of stars. A huge full moon sailed toward the mountain peaks in the west.

It was a perfect night for a wolf to prowl. An especially dangerous one had almost gotten her.

Or rather, Jassy told herself, she'd nearly *let* The Wolfman have her.

Her response to Seth was what had really frightened her. Difficult as he could be, he'd somehow managed to get under her skin. He challenged her usual good humor, aroused her anger and stirred her passions. The strength of desire she'd felt surprised her. Disturbed her.

How on earth was she going to maintain a comfortable distance between them from now on?

5

JASSY WORKED HARD over the next few days so she wouldn't dwell on the upcoming date with Seth. By Friday, in addition to her regular chores, she'd drilled a couple of lines of postholes and mowed the grounds around the enclosures. She'd also fixed the plumbing in her trailer and redecorated her living quarters with brightly printed fabric.

On Friday afternoon, while working on a rusty pump near the tame pack's enclosure, she was drawn into the interns' scent-rolling experiment.

"We should see what the wolves would do with perfume," Jassy overheard Keith say to Erin.

"I have a whole bottle of cologne I'd be more than happy to donate," Jassy volunteered.

Keith looked pleased. "That would be great."

"I'll run over to my trailer and get it for you," she offered.

The going-away gift from a friend in California held some sentimental value, but the exotic celebrity fragrance wasn't one Jassy would choose for herself. She preferred light or woodsy scents. Besides, she had to limit her possessions because she moved around so much. And, she reminded herself as she dug the bottle out of the saddlebag, she would be moving on in a couple of months.

Erin looked up from her notes when at Jassy's returned. Her eyes widened when she saw the bottle. "Erotic? Gee, that's pretty expensive. Isn't it one of those fancy perfumes they advertise on television?"

"I guess. But that's okay. Erotic may be the personal choice of movie stars, but it's not right for me."

Keith stuck his pen in his hair and motioned for the women to follow him around the corner of the enclosure. "Let's try it on a clean patch of grass. The other spot is saturated with non-toxic insect repellent."

"The wolves are, too," Erin said with a grimace. "They may roll in the cologne but it probably won't make them smell any better."

They remained outside the fence so the wolves would concentrate on scents rather than on greeting them. The pack lay quietly in the middle of the enclosure watching the three humans.

Jassy learned that Keith and Erin had determined that a wolf instinctually rolled in any new scent to which he was exposed, whether it was anchovy paste or lemon air-freshener. This behavior enabled wandering members to carry information back to the pack.

When Jassy reached through the wire to spray a dense layer of Erotic on the grass, Kaya immediately jumped up and ran toward her. As soon as she got a whiff of the new scent, the alpha female snorted and rolled. Geronimo and the others soon followed suit.

"Whew! That's kind of strong," Erin remarked when the wind direction shifted.

Keith seemed pleased. "Can't smell the insect repellent any more at all. I wonder how this type of cologne would work against skunk musk?"

Erin rolled her eyes. "You'll have to be the one to try that one, Keith."

Chuckling, Jassy glanced over her shoulder to see Seth approaching, his stride easy and graceful—and utterly masculine. Acutely aware of him, she quickly turned back to the experiment.

Big Bad's reaction was especially comical; everyone laughed as he waved his legs wildly in the air.

Seth came close enough to catch a whiff of the wolves. "Perfume? This enclosure smells like a brothel."

"Really?" Jassy quirked her eyebrows and gave him a sidelong glance. "And how many have you visited?"

Enigmatically, Seth didn't answer.

"Erotic sounds like a good choice for amorous ladies," Keith commented as he took the bottle from Jassy and inspected the label.

"Except the girls in this pen are pretty hairy," Jassy said, smiling. "Go ahead and keep that if you want to use cologne again."

Erin reached for the bottle and snatched it from Keith's hands. "I'll take it."

"Come on, Erin you just want to douse yourself, not the wolves," Keith complained.

"So what? They'll roll in anything."

The two continued arguing as Jassy walked back to continue work on the pump.

Seth followed her. "You've been putting in long hours," he observed.

Out of the corner of her eye, Jassy noticed every detail of his appearance. His hair was pulled back again with a leather tie, and he was wearing an old gray sweatshirt with the sleeves cut off, faded jeans and suede hiking boots. His expression was serious, his gaze penetrating. He looked both wild and dignified.

"My hours haven't been that long," Jassy insisted.

"How's your schedule for this afternoon?"

"I've got plenty of things to do," she said vaguely. He was probably going to ask her to make extra time for him.

"You won't be able to mow my lawn, then."

"Your lawn?" Feeling a little foolish at her assumption, she looked up at him. "No sweat. I'll mow it."

"Good. The weeds are so high, I can hardly see out the windows. I'd mow it myself if I didn't have some papers to finish filling out and a couple of lectures to prepare."

"What kind of lectures are you putting together, anyway?" A perennial student, Jassy was genuinely interested.

"What else? Wolf behavior and biology. I'm going to speak to a Seattle wilderness group next week. I might even be staying there for a few days."

"Sounds nice."

And Seth would be gone for a while, which would give her time to let her guard down. She'd have Saturday night to deal with first, though.

Or to look forward to, she amended as he walked off with a wave. Seth Heller had been difficult at times, but she'd learned to handle all types of people in her life. And she had to admit he'd let her have her space, hadn't pushed her once since the other night. She wasn't shy nor was she easily railroaded into doing things against her will. If she hadn't wanted to go out with Seth, she wouldn't have accepted his invitation in the first place.

She might as well admit the truth: She was looking forward to being with Seth almost as much as she dreaded the prospect.

HUNCHED OVER HIS DESK, Seth made another attempt at outlining his lecture on tame-pack social behavior compared to wild. But after several minutes of deep thought and pencil chewing, he'd come up with only one heading: Mating Rituals.

"Damn!" He crumpled the page he'd written on and threw it aside. He knew exactly what was haunting him.

Or rather, who.

He was obsessed with Jassy. No matter how hard he tried to avoid thinking about her, every time he went out the door, he immediately looked around to see what she was doing. And he'd been dreaming about blond hair, a dimpled smile and soft, tanned flesh night after night. Needless to say, he'd been waking up as hard as a randy teenager.

He tapped out a rapid beat with the pencil. He hadn't been this uptight over a female since he was sixteen. He should have dated more often during the past year, spent less time alone, because obviously the mere presence of an attractive woman was enough to strip his gears.

When the coughing sound of the power mower started up near the house, Seth almost jumped out of his skin. *Jassy.*

He forced himself to remain at the desk, his back toward the large windows that fronted the house. He'd been truthful when he'd said his lawn needed cutting badly. He hadn't been trying to find an excuse to get Jassy into closer proximity.

Seth tried to concentrate on the lecture. It wasn't long before he threw down the pencil and propped his chin on his hand. The memory of heated kisses and warm, taut breasts kept interfering with his concentration. Too bad Jassy wasn't ready to admit she desired him as much as he did her.

The mower droned on, the sound growing louder when Jassy neared the house, then fading as she moved away. She made several sweeps before the machine coughed again, ran rough, then died completely. Seth wasn't surprised. Like most of the refuge's equipment, the mower was old and touchy.

Figuring he might as well get it over with, he rose to take a look. But the sight that greeted him when he reached the plate-glass window was unexpected.

Jassy was leaning over the mower, her shirt pulled up, her lovely jeans-clad bottom pointed directly at the house. Admiring the sweet arc of her buttocks, the way she wiggled slightly as she tinkered with the machine, Seth could almost imagine she was beckoning to him. Her jeans had faded to a pale blue, and the darker central seam of the garment defined her firmly voluptuous cheeks.

His mouth went dry, and he immediately became aroused. Absently running a palm down his fly, he pressed hard against the growing tumescence that was making him uncomfortable. At that instant, Jassy straightened and glanced over her shoulder. She froze and her eyes widened.

Thinking there was no use torturing himself, Seth moved away from the window and threw himself into his chair at the desk.

WHEN SHE FINALLY GOT the mower working again, Jassy cut the grass with a vengeance. Unbelievable! Seth had had the gall to stand in the window and touch himself while he openly ogled her! How crude!

If he thought he was going to jump her or paw her tomorrow night, he had another think coming. Maybe she should just cancel. There should be something going on between two people besides lust. And she'd tell

him so to his face when she caught him peeping at her
again!

But he didn't make another appearance at the large
window in front or at any of the windows in back. Jassy
even stared up at the skylight on the roof to make sure
he wasn't perched up there. She was almost disappointed when she didn't see him.

Finishing her task in record time, she decided to give
Seth a piece of her mind.

She walked up to the front door and peered through
the glass panes. Like most small A-frames, the first floor
was a single huge room with a kitchen area at one end
and a two-story living room at the other. The second
level was a simple loft above the kitchen. Seth sat at a
desk near the open stairway that led upstairs. He didn't
even look up until Jassy tapped on the glass.

He rose and crossed to the door, which he quickly—
eagerly?—opened.

"Need something?"

No doubt he was referring to himself, Jassy thought
indignantly. The spark of interest in his gaze made her
go warm all over. Beyond diplomacy for once, she
pushed past him.

"I've been rethinking our plans for tomorrow," she
said tersely. "I don't want to date a man who's only interested in a physical relationship. We have to have
more in common than that."

Seth was surprised. "Who says we don't have anything in common?" He paused, then added reassur-

ingly, "If you're concerned because we got a little carried away the other night, don't be. It won't happen again unless *you* want it to."

His forthrightness disarmed her. "Well, I don't," she said, trying to convince herself it was true.

"All right. I can wait." His tone went from reassuring to provocative. "You can set the pace."

Her anger was dissipating, despite Seth's obvious certainty that she would eventually give him the go-ahead. Jassy realized she no longer had a point—not unless she was still willing to make an issue of his having stood at the window earlier, fingering his fly. And she was beginning to think he mightn't have been aware of it. He may have been responding to her unconsciously. Pure animal instinct.

Sounding too amused for her peace of mind, he assured her, "I don't force myself on women."

He was obviously implying that he didn't have to. Jassy knew that first hand. She hadn't exactly fought him off the other night. She'd have to watch herself tomorrow.

"As long as we have the physical part of the relationship straight," she muttered.

Fidgety with embarrassment, Jassy glanced about and noticed the tall bookcases lining one wall. She crossed to them, thinking she might as well inspect the place as long as she was there, make a bit of small talk so she'd feel comfortable enough to take her leave graciously.

"Like to read?" Seth asked. "I saw that pile of paper-backs in your trailer window."

"I read whenever I get the chance." Though she didn't usually peruse the sort of hardcover reference volumes lining Seth's shelves. "And I like maps."

She was referring to the ones decorating the walls. A framed, colorful map of Alaska hung on one side of the stone-and-mortar fireplace that had been built up through the steeply pitched roof. The framed map was more elaborate than the road maps Jassy always carried and marked up. A big map of Montana and Wyoming decorated the wall on the other side of the fireplace. Minnesota was stapled over his desk.

"Ever been to any of these places?" she asked, moving closer to examine Alaska.

Seth came up behind her. Her neck prickled.

"I've traveled most of the Western states," he told her. "And I've visited northern Minnesota and several parts of Alaska and Canada."

"To study wolves," she guessed, stepping away to look at the maps of Montana and Wyoming.

"And to see the country."

Seth followed her, keeping a barely respectable distance between them. Jassy could swear she felt his breath hot on her neck.

"You've never thought of living anywhere else?" she asked.

"Why should I? I like it here."

She could think of a good reason for him to leave and couldn't help needling him a bit after their discussion the other night. "Even though your neighbors hate you?"

"Ben and Ceil are the only neighbors who count. We get along real well." He slouched against the fireplace and folded his arms across his chest as he switched the discussion to her. "Why do you like to move around so much, anyway?"

"I'm seeing the country, too," Jassy explained, noting the way Seth's cutoff sweatshirt revealed his tanned, muscular arms. "Going on three years now."

"I'd think you'd run out of states after a while."

She grinned. "Then I'll revisit them."

"So how long do you stay in each place?"

Her grin faded to an annoyed grimace. He certainly was full of questions. She stepped over to his desk and gazed at the map of Minnesota. The northern counties—wolf territory—were outlined in blue marker.

"I don't keep track of how long I stay anywhere," she said. "I'm usually too busy doing interesting things. I move on when I'm ready—sometimes a couple of weeks, sometimes several months."

"Don't you miss anyone . . . like your mother?"

Jassy had never said she and her mother were close. Turning, she frowned at him. "I see Mom every once in a while. I have some stuff stored at her place in Ohio."

"But you didn't want to settle down there with her?"

"I have no intentions of settling anywhere. Hey, why don't you give me a questionnaire to fill out? I feel like I'm being grilled."

"Can't I be curious about someone who interests me?"

Accustomed to justifying her life-style, Jassy told herself Seth was no different from the others who'd questioned it, so she shouldn't be so uptight. "I've never found a place I wanted to live permanently," she explained. "As far as I'm concerned, there's nothing like being footloose and fancy-free."

"Though you must get lonely?"

She'd indeed had her bouts of loneliness, but she wasn't about to discuss something so personal with him. "I have friends all across the country."

"More like, friendly acquaintances."

"Friends," she repeated unequivocally, not surprised that Seth would have limited ideas of what friendship meant.

"Still, it takes a special type of personality to live the way you do."

"And what type is that?"

"A loner."

Jassy bridled. "What on earth gives you that idea? You're the lone wolf, not me."

Seth straightened and pushed away from the fireplace. "Maybe there're two kinds of lone wolves, then. I'm the type who has a territory."

"I'm not *any* kind of loner," she insisted again. "I might be by myself sometimes, but I'm not antisocial."

"And I am?" Seth smiled wryly as he moved closer. "Well, to some extent, you're right about that. I only brought up the lone-wolf idea because I thought that was something we had in common."

Jassy felt trapped against the desk. Not that Seth was touching her in any way. He merely made his presence felt, made her respond whether or not she wanted to. Her stomach tightened and she felt distinctly edgy. Trying to ignore the attraction that was beginning to seem as natural to her as breathing, Jassy changed the subject. She refused to argue about her own life-style any longer.

"So you regard Wolf's Lair as your territory?" She realized Seth frequently made wolf references to himself. "Even though Ben Lasky owns the place?"

"He's added my name to the deed. I'd think of this neck of the woods as home, anyway," he went on. "I've lived on this land since I graduated from high school. I used to have an old one-room shack behind the Laskys' cabin."

Seth and the Laskys must be even closer than she thought. "Your quarters have certainly improved," she said, taking that opportunity to move away from Seth.

Feeling an immediate surge of relief once she'd put a few feet between them, Jassy took a better look around. While the house was probably only a few years old, the furniture was surely secondhand. Everything looked so cozy—the couch and chairs arranged around the fireplace, the worn rug, the big desk stacked with papers. And she'd bet Seth had put the bookcases together himself.

Scattered around the room were a couple of Eskimo carvings, a few Native American artifacts, some driftwood and seashells. Each item was obviously intended to please the owner rather than impress his guests.

"I guess you could call my cycle my home," Jassy said, feeling oddly defensive although Seth hadn't brought the subject up again.

She glanced up at his loft where a mattress and box spring were placed beneath the skylight. He must be able to gaze out at the stars at night. Tempted to crawl up there to see for herself, she grew even more restless.

She glanced out the windows and noticed that dusk had fallen. "I should be going."

"And I have some work I need to finish," Seth said.

Crossing the area near the desk, she kicked a crumpled sheet of paper that lay on the floor. She picked it up, smoothed it out and read the heading.

"'Mating Rituals'?" She handed the page to Seth. "Your notes?"

"Part of my lecture."

Jassy wasn't sure. She couldn't help being titillated by the idea that Seth mightn't have been thinking of wolves when he'd written the heading. Then she grew annoyed with herself, especially when she realized he was staring at her.

"Usually the alpha pair are the only ones to mate in a pack," he told her. "And the female chooses exactly when and where."

Just as Seth had told her she could set the pace? "How interesting," she murmured, edging toward the door. "Well, I really should be going." She smiled nervously as he moved closer to her.

"You already said that." Seth opened the door for her. "See you tomorrow night."

"Right."

Outside, Jassy jogged toward her trailer. They'd have a good time, she assured herself. They did have interests in common and she certainly couldn't complain about Seth's looks. She liked him, challenging though he was. She only wished she felt less jittery when they were together. Already leery of their intense physical attraction, she resented his prying into her personal life.

But he'd been dead wrong about her being a loner.

Jassy had never sought solitude. It wasn't her fault that her family had moved from place to place, making it difficult for her to have long-term friends. Nor could she blame herself for failing to feel close to her parents who'd wanted their children to play traditional roles. Dieter had gone along with tradition, and he'd been lost to her. If she'd had her choice in the matter, her brother would never have joined the marines.

At least she'd found ways to make the best of things, combating personal tragedy by establishing friendships wherever she went and focusing on the positive qualities in people and her current environment. She considered herself a child of the universe; the whole world was her home.

Attempting to enjoy the beauty that surrounded her right now, Jassy slowed her pace, breathing in pine-fragrant air. Violet shadows lengthened beneath bushes and trees as the sun sank beyond the mountains. Venus hung like a small glowing jewel in the sky. How gorgeous! The moon would be rising soon, although the clouds gathering on the horizon probably meant the night would be dark and stormy. But rain was also okay. Jassy loved to read to the sound of raindrops.

Hurrying to her trailer, she glimpsed a slight movement in the wild-pack enclosure and turned to see a shadowy form half-hidden by a pile of logs.

"Lucifer!"

The silver-tipped dark wolf nodded his head as if greeting her. He stared at Jassy with amber eyes.

Startled by the wolf's resemblance to his master, she stopped, compelled to say, "Hey, guy, you're ogling the wrong species. I only go out with two-legged wolves." But Lucifer took off, presumably to return to his pack.

Feeling a sudden need for some sort of companionship herself, Jassy walked past the trailer and checked the veterinary building and the equipment shed to see if Erin and Keith were still around. They had left, but the lights glimmered from the Lasky cabin beyond on the rise. Ceil had told Jassy she was always welcome to visit them.

Deciding she didn't want to bother the older couple at their supper hour, Jassy headed back for the trailer. Used to coping on her own, she'd fix herself something to eat and lose herself in a novel. And that action would be solitary rather than antisocial, she assured herself.

Not that Seth would know the difference.

6

THE NEXT MORNING, Jassy visited Ceil and was invited
to come back for the noon meal. Seth would be there,
as well.

Jassy finished her morning duties, cleaned up and
started for the Laskys' place a little early. When she
stepped outside her trailer, she noticed unusual behavior in the tame-pack enclosure nearby.

Snowbird huddled tightly against the fence staring
longingly at Jassy. Beyond her the other females paced
back and forth restlessly, growling loudly.

Frowning, Jassy approached and knelt beside the
fence. "What's the matter, baby?" she crooned, pushing her hand inside the wire to pat the shivering wolf.
She'd gone out of her way to establish a relationship
with Snowbird, who was still an outcast. "Don't let
those bullies get to you. You have a right to be here,
too."

The wolf whined. She seemed so sad and lost, Jassy
felt like crying. And she was worried about the aggres-
siveness of the other females. She'd ask Seth about
moving Snowbird the minute she saw him.

But Seth hadn't arrived yet when Jassy reached the
Lasky cabin. Ceil was busy preparing what seemed to

be a gargantuan meal while being watched closely by several cats and a couple of dogs. She told Jassy to sit down at the table and make herself at home.

"Surely I can do something," said Jassy, not wanting to be waited on.

Ceil was frying several chicken pieces in a huge skillet. "You can get the stuff out of the refrigerator if you'd like. It's in there." She waved a hand toward the aging appliance sitting in the pantry. "The potato salad's on the top shelf, the jelly salad's on the bottom, and there's butter in the inside drawer." Then she gently shook off a striped cat who'd slid his paws around her ankle. "Get out of here, Thomas, you pig! You'll get your chicken later."

Jassy laughed, arranging the two salad dishes and the plate of butter on the table. There was already a platter of fresh corn on the cob and another of homemade rolls. The entire house smelled fragrant; Ceil must have baked bread that morning.

Ceil was bringing the chicken to the table when Ben and Seth came in. They washed up at the sink before sitting down.

Jassy immediately broached her concerns. "There's something going on with the tame pack. The other females are acting like they want to beat up on Snowbird."

Seth nodded. "I think Kaya is going into heat again. That's why the others are nervous."

"As long as Snowbird stays out of their way, she'll be all right," Ben said.

"Are you sure?" Jassy gazed from one man to the other. "Those animals are growling and showing their teeth."

"Pack rituals rarely become life-threatening," Seth declared. "Besides, Erin and Keith arrived before I came in. They'll be watching."

Jassy was reassured. Both men had had years of experience and surely knew what they were talking about. She knew wolves didn't make good pets, still, she wished she could put Snowbird in the trailer to keep her safe.

Seth patted the two Lasky dogs, a golden retriever and a curly-haired mutt. Thomas, set on trying someone else in his quest for chicken, also got a pat when he brushed against Seth's leg.

So far, Jassy had seen two gray cats, a spotted one, an orange tabby and a half-grown black kitten. Obviously animal lovers, the Laskys also had a rather moth-eaten macaw on a big perch at one end of the kitchen.

When Jassy glanced at him, the parrot raised his beak and cried, "Woo-o-o-ohh!"

She chuckled. "Has he been listening to the wolves?"

"That feathered idiot repeats everything," Ben grumbled.

Ceil laughed. "Raoul especially likes swearwords." She gazed at her husband, "And you give him plenty to choose from, dear."

Ben grunted and helped himself to a couple of pieces of chicken and a big serving of potato salad. "Ceil is the one who collects strays, not me," he told Jassy.

"And the biggest stray was *you*." Ceil's lively dark eyes twinkled. Probably in her late sixties, she was plump and attractive. "Twenty-five years ago, when this cabin had only one room, I found Ben passed out on the floor, sick from exhaustion. I splashed some water on his face, fixed a decent meal for him, fed his wolves—"

"And moved in," growled Ben, finishing the sentence for her.

Ceil punched her husband lightly in the arm. "I didn't move in until we were married."

"You were just waiting to get your hooks into me." Ben's grumpy tone was obviously good-natured teasing.

"Hooks?" Ceil raised her eyebrows. "I was worried about you, that's all. You were working nearly twenty-four hours a day, what with the wolves and those two jobs you had. If I hadn't come along, I don't know what you would have done."

"Probably stayed single," Ben said, winking at Jassy.

Ceil punched him again. "Probably ended up dead from overwork is more like it."

Grinning, Seth gazed at Jassy as he passed her the chicken, then the rolls. "They deserve each other, as you can tell."

Jassy laughed. Seth was much more relaxed in this setting.

"So Wolf's Lair was a one-man operation to begin with," she noted. So Ben, who must be seventy-something, had married late in life.

"It all began when Ben took in six wolves from a ninety-year-old man upstate," Seth explained. "The guy was sick and had been advertising in the paper, hoping someone would provide a good home for the animals. Ben was interested in wildlife and owned some land."

"It was a damned hard struggle, though," Ben said between mouthfuls of food. "I was working for a logging company off and on, and when I couldn't get enough days there, I took another job at a fish cannery."

"Then I moved into the area," Ceil continued the story. "I was from Seattle originally, and wanted a change of scenery after my divorce. Being used to a city, I was real lonesome and tried visiting my neighbors. I noticed Ben was in trouble when I dropped by a couple of times." She laughed. "I *had* to marry the old fogey and pick up an extra job to make sure that he and the wolves had enough to eat."

Ben snorted. "You already had to work an extra job to feed all those cats and dogs you owned." He glanced around, spotting Thomas begging beside his chair. He gave the cat a sliver of chicken. "We've still got—what is it—eight of these mangy felines around here."

"And a parrot, two dogs, three miniature goats and two raccoons," Seth pointed out.

"The goats and raccoons are out back, Jassy," Ceil said.

But Jassy was watching Seth. She noticed his softer-than-normal expression and wondered if bighearted Ceil had had a hand in taming him, as well. If he'd lived on the refuge since graduating from high school, he and the older couple must have known each other for quite some time. The three shared a warm camaraderie and affection that Jassy couldn't help but envy. She wondered about Seth's real parents.

"I only took the baby raccoons because their mother was killed in a trap," Ceil went on. "I had to feed them milk from a bottle. I plan to set them free in another week or so." She looked at Jassy. "Think you might like to come along? We could drive them up into the mountains."

Looking forward to an outing as well as a chance to spend more time with the older woman, Jassy smiled. "I'd love to go."

Joking and making small talk about the history of the area, the group settled down to some serious eating. Jassy gave away quite a bit of her chicken when Thomas, the black kitten and both dogs performed begging acts.

"Watch out," Seth teased. "They'll eat everything on your plate if you let them. They're professionals."

Jassy smiled, wishing Seth were this happy all the time.

Later, Ceil and Jassy stacked the dishes in the old-fashioned sink. It had an attached porcelain drainboard and a homemade fabric skirt that hid the drainpipe. Jassy figured Ceil had probably made the matching window curtains, as well. The cabin was rambling and even cozier than Seth's house.

"You built on the rest of the rooms after you got married, right?" Jassy asked Ceil.

"Uh-hmm. The last addition went on the summer Seth started helping out." Ceil wrinkled her brow in concentration. "Let's see, that must have been about twenty years ago."

Twenty? That would have made Seth around fifteen. "I thought Seth started living out here after he graduated from high school." In his own separate place, of course. Seth was the type who obviously cherished independence.

"Ben put Seth to work several years before he moved onto the refuge." Noticing Jassy's curiosity, Ceil lowered her voice so that Seth wouldn't hear. "Has Seth told you about his background?"

"Some."

"I figured so. I'll tell you more about it another time," Ceil promised.

Jassy was intrigued. What else would she learn about The Wolfman?

When Ceil served fresh apple pie, Ben closed his eyes on the first mouthful, savoring the flavor. "Damned good, as usual."

"And you certainly didn't have cooking like this when you were single," commented Ceil. "You should be grateful I came along at all." She winked and leaned closer to touch her husband's cheek. "You even got some side benefits I won't embarrass you by mentioning."

Ben coughed and turned red while everyone else laughed.

Ceil winked at Jassy. "It takes a special sort of man to handle wolves—and a special sort of woman to handle a wolf man. The only problem is, these bohunks don't realize they need anyone at all."

Seth disagreed. "No matter what he says, Ben would lock you up if you tried to leave, Ceil."

Ben coughed again, and Ceil chuckled. "I know that." She shook her fork at Seth. "But it's time you found a woman for yourself. Don't wait until you're fifty to settle down, like he did. You should have kids."

Seth made no comment but he didn't appear annoyed with the lecture.

"Not that those floozies you used to date would make good wives," Ceil continued in her outspoken fashion. "You need someone who's kind and sensitive, who loves the forest and animals."

Ceil looked directly at Jassy.

And Jassy looked down at her plate to scrape up a bit of nonexistent pie. Surely Ceil wasn't referring to her. She didn't want to settle down in one place at the moment, much less get married. And she hardly knew Seth.

Ceil quickly changed the topic. "There's supposed to be a big windstorm blowing in tonight. That's another reason the wolves could be restless. Those animals pick up on any changes in the air."

"You might be right," Ben agreed.

Deciding she'd like to check on Snowbird again, Jassy thanked Ceil for the meal. "It was really wonderful. Can I help with the dishes?"

"Go on," Ceil told her. "You've done enough."

"I'll have to cook the next time we get together," Jassy promised with a bright smile. After all, she enjoyed the Laskys' company. "I could make something exotic." Something she'd learned during her travels. "Stir-fry, shish kebob, paella, sushi."

Ben frowned. "Sushi? Isn't that some kind of raw fish gunk?"

"Marinated fish," Jassy corrected.

"Whatever." Ben complained, "I hate fish unless you bread 'em and fry the hell out of them."

Ceil punched his arm. "Don't quarrel with people who offer you hospitality. He'll eat anything you fix, Jassy."

Jassy paused on the plank porch to scan the horizon for storm clouds.

Seth came out of the cabin a split second later. "How about six o'clock?" When she didn't respond immediately, he continued, "I can drive by and pick you up at six o'clock this evening, all right?"

Oh, the date. "Fine," Jassy agreed.

Her mind hadn't been on their outing, which was surprising, considering how much time she'd spent trying to ignore it all week.

"I'm not sure what movie is playing," he told her. "We'll have to look at the paper. I think it's some kind of action adventure."

"I like movies of all types, particularly action adventure." That kind of film would probably be fast-paced, and Jassy wouldn't be so aware of the attractive man sitting beside her, wouldn't dwell on the way he kissed.

"Then we can either eat at a café or the pizzeria. Do you have a preference?"

"Any kind of food is fine with me." She appreciated Seth's thoughtfulness in giving her choices.

She also appreciated his letting her set the pace for their date. Now, if she could only figure out how to control her own reactions, she'd feel a whole lot better. Too many things about The Wolfman—his earthiness, his strength, his air of cool mystery—appealed to Jassy on a very basic level.

"How about walking back to the enclosure to take a look at Snowbird?" Seth asked.

"The sooner the better," she urged, stepping off the porch. At least she could trust both herself and Seth where taking care of animals was concerned.

HE'D PLAYED DOWN his concern to Jassy, but Seth was also disturbed by the way the females were behaving.

Even the male wolves had become restless by mid-afternoon, snarling and hassling each other. The pack was more uptight than Seth had ever seen them, threatening the possibility of a major shake-up, which could result in a new alpha male or female—or both. But if he removed Snowbird or any of the other low-ranking animals, he was afraid they'd never again be allowed into the pack.

Seth decided to hang around and keep an eye on things. As soon as Jassy left to do some work on the fence, he asked Keith and Erin if either would be able to stay in the observation tower that evening. Keith agreed, promising to yell for Ben if he needed help. If necessary, when he returned with Jassy, Seth would take the midnight shift himself.

He was in the veterinary building a few minutes later when all hell broke loose: Keith's hoarse shouts and Erin's cries mixed with the sounds of growling and snarling wolves. His heart pounding, Seth dropped the box of supplies he'd been carrying and took off running.

As he raced toward the enclosure, he saw Snowbird running ahead of the pack. Kaya and Moon, the beta female, were nipping at her heels with powerful jaws. A streak of blood already stained Snowbird's white coat.

"Get between them!" Erin yelled at Keith as he chased the animals, a fire extinguisher in his hands.

"I'm trying!" Keith shouted, attempting to head Kaya and Moon off.

But the animals were so fast, they'd be lucky if they hit them with the extinguisher foam, much less keep them from fighting.

Grabbing an extinguisher himself—the chemical was usually effective in discouraging the animals' aggressive behavior—Seth opened the gate and latched it behind him before entering the melee. He ran toward the end of the enclosure where Kaya and Moon had cornered Snowbird under a log.

"Hey, hey, stop it!" Seth yelled, trying to circumvent Kaya as the alpha female charged forward.

Like any wolf who is angry with another, Kaya paid no attention to Seth and dodged him easily. He was perfectly safe, since she had no quarrel with him. She would attack only the object of her wrath.

Snowbird received a slicing bite to her hindquarters that sent her scrambling out from under the log.

"Kaya!" Seth shouted to get the alpha female's attention.

To no avail. Kaya leaped over the log to chase Snowbird into a frontal attack by Moon. The beta female nearly brought the white wolf down.

But Snowbird feinted to the side while Seth and Erin blasted Moon liberally with the extinguishers, driving her off. Keith was working against Kaya, who also backed away.

"Chill out!" Keith shouted, shooting foam at the alpha female.

Nobody noticed Natane, one of the juvenile females, until the young wolf had zoomed in for her own attack on Snowbird. Protecting herself, the white wolf snarled and ripped into the younger one savagely, drawing blood. Erin aimed the foam at Snowbird, temporarily blinding her.

Unfortunately. At that very moment, Kaya rushed in again, bringing Snowbird down. The alpha wolf pinned the white wolf and took hold of her throat.

Seth froze. He was certain Kaya was going to kill Snowbird. Focusing on the tableau before him, he caught a hint of moving color as someone else entered the wolf enclosure.

"No, no!" screamed Jassy, running straight for the two wolves.

7

"NO, KAYA! NO-O-O!" Jassy shrieked again as she plunged across the pen. She wouldn't allow Snowbird to die! "No!"

Throwing herself at Kaya, Jassy knocked the wolf to the ground and broke her hold. Snowbird scrambled away and Kaya squirmed out from under Jassy, both wolves then streaking toward the opposite end of the enclosure.

Desperate, Jassy chased after them, running faster than she would ever have believed she could. Somehow she managed to corner Kaya by the water trough.

"*I said no!*" Jassy yelled.

She grabbed the snarling alpha female by the scruff of her neck. Too furious to be afraid or to doubt her strength, she dragged the eighty-pound wolf to the trough and dumped her in the water.

"No, you will not harm Snowbird! Not ever! If you so much as try, I'll . . . I'll throttle you!"

With only her head and a single thrashing leg above the water line, Kaya tried to climb out of the shallow trough several times but Jassy held her firmly in place.

"No! Chill out!"

Intent on keeping Kaya in check, Jassy was unaware of the other activity around her until Seth took hold of her shoulder. She jumped and whipped around to face him. She was breathing hard.

"Settle down, Jassy," he said soothingly, stroking her the same way he would gentle an animal. "Snowbird's safe. We've already got her out of here, and Keith's calling the vet."

"Is Snowbird hurt badly?"

"Her injuries don't look as bad as Natane's. And I'm sure some of the other wolves have bites that need to be treated."

Her adrenaline surge ebbing, her emotions in flux, Jassy let Kaya go. She wanted to sag to the ground with exhaustion but she forced herself to remain upright. Behind her, splashing noises told her Kaya was climbing out of the trough. She turned and glared at the wet wolf, who slinked off.

"Can you help Erin check the pack for injuries?" Seth asked hurriedly. "I need to carry Natane to the veterinary building."

Jassy nodded. "Of course."

Seth picked up the injured wolf and strode away. Jassy and Erin got busy inspecting the wolves, though some were so agitated, they ran from the humans. At least it was a sign they weren't seriously hurt.

Big Bad had a bloody ear and three of the females had minor bites that would have to be treated. Kaya had suffered little physical harm but she immediately became distraught when Jassy approached. The wolf flattened herself to the ground and crawled alongside the fence on her belly.

"What's the matter with her?"

Erin made a wry face. "She's afraid you're going to kill her."

Jassy swallowed, feeling guilty as she remembered threatening to throttle the animal. "I was just angry and upset."

"But your really sounded like you meant it. You showed your dominance over her, and believe me, Kaya isn't going to forget that for a long time."

Nor would Jassy forget the horrible snarling battle that had been going on when she leaped into the enclosure. Though Seth had told her they were noble beasts and more civilized than many humans, wolves were also capable of warfare.

Worse, Jassy realized that she herself was capable of hurtful violence in the heat of the moment. She wasn't sure how far she would have gone if Kaya had dared to resist her.

THE STORM BUILT on the horizon late in the afternoon. Dark clouds shrouded the peaks to the west. Jassy, busy with Ben, Ceil and the others, didn't worry about rain or wind.

Charlie Metcalf, the vet, and his wife, Fay, arrived to treat the injured wolves. Snowbird's wounds looked awful but didn't require stitches. Natane, on the other hand, had a gaping tear in her side. The yearling wolf had lost so much blood, she needed to be taken to the Metcalfs' infirmary for an overnight stay. As a safety precaution, Seth climbed in the back of the vet's van to accompany the wolf and get her settled in.

Jassy watched them drive away, then returned to the veterinary building to help clean up.

A bit later, after everyone else had scattered, Jassy visited the enclosure. When Kaya sighted her, she flattened herself and crept away into the shadows. Feeling terribly guilty again, Jassy leaned against the fence.

"I'm sorry, Kaya!" she called into the darkness. "I won't harm you. I don't want to harm anybody or anything, honestly."

Not that the wolf could understand.

Only part of the enclosure was lit by the security lights, but Jassy thought she could see most of the pack huddled together near their flat-topped shelter, no doubt in preparation for the coming storm. At least Kaya had company. Poor Snowbird was all by herself. Jassy found the white wolf lying inside a smaller shelter in one of the individual pens that shared the wild pack's fence line.

"Hello, baby," she murmured, opening the gate to go inside. She lowered herself to the ground to pet Snowbird's matted fur. The wolf flinched when she touched a sore spot. Jassy's eyes filled with tears. "Don't you worry, you'll get well. And you'll be okay. You're a child of the universe, like me. You don't need a home." Especially not a place where a bunch of other hostile inhabitants made her feel unwelcome. Jassy had had that experience plenty of times herself.

The moon overhead would soon be obliterated by clouds. The rising wind whipped through the surrounding trees, creating a haunting, soughing sound as pine branches rubbed together. Thunder rumbled and one of the wolves in the wild pack howled. Snowbird pricked her ears and whined. Howling was a social activity; the whole pack often joined in.

"I'll be your packmate, Snowbird," Jassy told her. Then she cupped her mouth and looked up at the sky. "*A-a-w-oo-o!*"

Snowbird sat up and began with her own howl. "*A-a-w-oo-o...*"

"*Oo-o-h-h...*"

"*A-w-w-w...*"

And then the whole refuge erupted in a cacophony of howls. The wild, sweet cries of both wolf packs seemed to express the very soul of loneliness. It seemed to Jassy that they were saying that no one could understand, no one could help, no one would be waiting at the end of the road.

Jassy understood perfectly.

She'd wandered all her life and would probably continue to do so. Alone. Forever. Her heart aching, she finally allowed her pent-up tears to fall. As her howl turned into a sob, she leaned back against Snowbird's shelter.

A shadow fell across the pen.

Startled, Jassy glanced up to see Seth opening the gate. She swiped the back of her hand across her eyes so he wouldn't see that she'd been crying. He came inside and, before she could get up, knelt to take her in his arms. Unable to stop herself, Jassy began to sob again at his tender gesture.

Whispering soothing words, Seth nestled her against his chest, kissing and stroking her hair. "Don't worry. Everything's going to be all right."

His flannel shirt felt soft against her cheek. His arms were steady and rock hard and comforting. She slid her hands around his waist and held on for dear life. He pulled her around so they sat with their backs against the shelter.

"We took care of Natane," he told her. "She'll be fine. All the animals will be fine."

Jassy took a deep, shuddering breath of relief. "Why didn't you take Snowbird out of the enclosure long ago?" she asked. "How could you have let something so awful happen?"

"I've never seen a shake-up go this far before. Wolves don't normally try to kill each other."

"Who says?"

"Books, researchers." Seth paused. "Except, most studies have been based on wild packs with plenty of territory. In that type of situation, the omega wolf could be driven away. Poor Snowbird was trapped."

"Then you should have removed her," Jassy insisted, as anger replaced her tears.

"Even though doing so would have made it impossible for her to ever relate to the pack again?" he pointed out, his voice sad. "We were hoping she'd be accepted. Now she has to be caged alone."

Snowbird really was a lone wolf now, Jassy thought.

She pulled away to check on her. The white wolf had crawled back into her shelter to lie down. Seth remained where he was, and again draped one arm loosely around Jassy's shoulders.

"Poor baby," she mourned for Snowbird, her anger tinged with sorrow. "This wasn't her fault."

"Things happen."

"Unfair things!"

"Unfortunately, life isn't fair."

"But you're supposed to be tough enough to spit back in life's face, right?"

Seth could tell Jassy was still upset, though she'd managed to stanch her tears. The wolf incident had triggered a deep emotional reaction that had to be the result of long-buried personal issues.

"No one can be tough all the time," he assured her, stroking her hair.

"A soldier is. A soldier should be hard as nails."

"But you're not a soldier."

"My father thought Dieter and I were his own special task force," Jassy said bitterly. "We were raised to keep our barracks neat, our shoulders straight and our rifles ready. You can see where that got my brother."

"You really miss him."

"He was the only person I could talk to . . . most of the time. Even that changed after he joined the marines. I was on my own."

"No wonder you hate violence and war."

"War?" Jassy stared at him. "I hated the entire military system before I knew what war was. All that posturing and rank stuff gave me the creeps."

"Your mother mustn't have liked it, either," he said, since Jassy had told him her parents were divorced.

"Ha! You're wrong. My mother loved being an officer's wife even more than she loved my father. She thought I should follow her example—become a regular little lady with gloves and a hat. All I wanted was to get as far away from the military as possible as soon as I got the chance."

"And you succeeded."

"Sort of." Jassy sighed. "Wolf packs are too rank-conscious and warlike for my comfort."

In defense of the animals, Seth explained, "I told you they probably wouldn't have gone this far if they were in a natural environment. And their behavior is instinctual and serves to protect and maintain the group as a whole."

"Just as armies are supposed to protect and maintain society? At least wolves have the excuse of possessing a few less brains than humans."

Cynical about his own species, Seth raised his brows. "Are you sure about that?" He grinned wryly.

"You don't even have to be in the military to be mean and nasty," Jassy murmured. "When I was growing up, I met plenty of crummy kids."

"You must have been the new kid in class over and over. So many people fear and hate the new or different. Age doesn't matter."

She gazed at him, curious. "You were different, too, weren't you? Why?"

"Maybe it had something to do with my mother and the way folks around here treated her." Seth didn't intend to go into detail, but he figured Jassy would hear soon enough. "My mother was the town drunk."

"If you were treated badly because of your mother, that's even worse. People took out their prejudices on you. I don't know how human beings can be so stupid and inhumane."

Seth didn't answer. No one except Ceil and Ben had come to his defense before. When a raindrop hit his forehead, he glanced up at the sky.

"It's going to pour," Jassy said as the rain began pelting down. "We'd better get inside."

She wobbled a little as he helped her up. He kept a firm hold on her as they left the pen. By the time they reached her trailer, the wind was whipping sheets of rain across the open areas of the refuge and bursts of lightning split the sky. Thunder crashed and rumbled.

They were both soaked. Wet tendrils of Jassy's hair clung to her face and shoulders. She grabbed a couple of towels out of the cupboard and handed one to Seth. He blotted his face and beard and watched her. A towel might dry her face and her arms but in her long-sleeved T-shirt her pretty, round breasts were exposed in erect-nippled detail.

Since it was too late to go to a movie in Pineville, Seth wondered if she was anxious to get rid of him.

But when she turned toward him, he realized her mind was still on their conversation.

"As least my background taught me to handle people, nasty or not. You never tell people your troubles. Nobody wants to hear anything bad," she said. "Positive and funny goes a lot further. Give them a dose of that and a little personal interest and you can have anyone eating out of your hand."

"For a while, maybe." Seth's heart went out to her. Her blue eyes were vulnerable, yet defiant.

"So what? All I need is *a while*."

"If you want to settle for short-term friendships."

Her face flushed. "And what do you know about friendships?"

"I have two long-term friends I can say anything to."

"Ben and Ceil." Jassy dried her hands as if she could wipe away unpleasant thoughts. She finally spoke in a low voice, "I used to be able to say anything to Dieter."

"And you can say anything to me if you want," he offered. "I can make a pretty good guess at your real feelings, anyway. You might as well be open about them."

She blinked and shook her head. "But what if *I* don't want to know what I'm feeling?"

He stepped closer to cup her chin so she'd look at him. "Why wouldn't you want to know? Feelings aren't wrong."

"No, just terribly angry... or sad."

Her lips trembled, then her eyes filled. She grimaced and tried to pull away.

Unwilling to let her escape, Seth enveloped her in his arms. Jassy pushed at him a couple of times, then finally capitulated, leaning against his chest the same way she had in Snowbird's pen. She was crying quietly and trying to hide it.

"Don't be embarrassed," he told her gruffly. "You aren't the only one who's had a few rounds with loneliness and hurt." He'd do anything he could to take away the pain she was feeling.

Jassy's reply was muffled. "I d-don't know what's the matter with me."

Seth stroked her back. "Maybe you let your sadness build up for too long. Maybe you ran away from it." Probably as fast as she'd left people and places behind.

"Who wouldn't run away from acting like an idiot?" She sniffed and wiped her cheek with her hand.

"I don't think you're an idiot." He pulled a handkerchief out of his pocket and handed it to her. "And now that you've faced everything squarely, I bet you'll feel like a different person in the morning."

He wished he could stay all night to make sure. He still wanted to protect—and possess—Jassy.

"You're feeling better right now, aren't you?" he asked.

She kept her gaze downward. "Yeah, I guess so."

"You should. You should respect yourself. It takes guts to open up the way you have." He trailed a finger along her jaw.

She smiled tremulously. "So I'm a good little soldier, hmm?"

"Better. You're great, Jassy. I'm learning to appreciate the real woman beneath all those happy-go-lucky smiles."

She looked up at him, her lips half parted, her eyes speaking volumes.

"There's no reason to hide—not ever," Seth murmured. "You're beautiful, inside and out."

Jassy's voice was soft as her expression. "What a nice thing to say."

"It's the truth."

Jassy slid an arm around his neck and kissed his cheek, then drew back for an instant before placing her lips over his. The kiss deepened and she pressed herself full-length against him.

Unable to resist such an overt assault, Seth kissed her in return, although he was careful to hold himself in check, not knowing what she expected.

And maintaining control wasn't easy, considering he was aware of every soft curve. Jassy's breasts invited, her thighs beckoned, and all the while her tongue played hide-and-seek with his, brushing lightly against his teeth and the roof of his mouth. He wound his fingers through her damp hair and breathed in her wonderful scent. She sighed and rubbed herself sensually against him.

Hell, control was going to be next to impossible, Seth realized as his heart raced and his body switched into high gear. But logic warned him to be careful of Jassy's fragile emotional state. She might be reaching out for whoever happened to be nearby. He wanted her to want *him*—not just anyone who could make her feel better.

"Jassy," he said softly when she broke the kiss for a moment. "Don't drive me crazy like this unless you intend to continue."

"Okay."

She then melded her mouth to his again.

Did that mean she wanted to make love? Nearly lost in the sensations she stirred in him, Seth closed his eyes as she slipped both arms about his waist and lowered her hand to caress his hip. He caught his breath. "Jassy!"

This time she didn't answer. Pulling his shirt out of his jeans, she slid her palms across his bare back. He trembled as he anchored her pelvis against his burgeoning hardness.

Jassy moaned. She unfastened his belt buckle, then started on his zipper.

On fire, Seth picked her up before she could finish and sat her down on the built-in counter behind them. He kissed her throat and wedged himself between her legs. But she was wearing jeans, not a skirt and he was going to have to get them off first....

"The bed," Jassy murmured, unbuttoning his shirt. "It'll be more comfortable."

Her words penetrated Seth's foggy mind. He pulled back. "Bed?" His breath was labored. "Are you sure you know what you're doing? In another minute, we won't be able to stop." He'd told her she could set the pace, but he wasn't sure that she was capable of making any such decision at the moment.

"Who wants to stop?" Jassy's eyes were cloudy, her lips moist.

"I don't want to take advantage of you." And he wanted to make sure it was *him* she desired, not a convenient warm body. He realized that more than his passion had been aroused by their earlier conversation. Her revelations had touched him deeply, and he wanted all of her.

Gripping her by the arms, Seth put Jassy away from him. "This isn't right. You're still upset." Reluctantly he announced, "I should leave."

Her eyes widened. "You're leaving?"

"Unless we can both cool down." He backed away from the counter. "It's not that I don't want you. But this isn't the best time."

Jassy slid down from the counter and moved away from him. "Maybe you *should* go."

"Or else we could have a cup of coffee and talk some more," Seth suggested. He really didn't want to leave her.

"We've talked enough."

She sounded so hurt and defensive, he took the risk of touching her. He stroked her face.

"Don't feel rejected," he murmured. "I do want you."

She lowered her eyes. "I know."

"But I think we ought to wait until you're in a better place emotionally."

She nodded hesitantly. "Um...thanks for lending me your shoulder."

"My pleasure. Talk to me anytime. You could stand to have someone steady around," he said, knowing it was true from experience. "Moving from place to place and person to person will never make things any different for you. You need commitment."

She smiled shyly.

But when Jassy didn't come up with any other response, Seth figured she wasn't ready to discuss her needs yet. He buttoned his shirt and turned toward the door.

"Good night, then."

"Good night."

"Are you sure you'll be all right?" he asked.

She met his gaze. "Absolutely. Thanks for asking."

"See you tomorrow."

With one last glance at her, he plunged out into the storm. The rain was cold, but he felt warm inside as he sprinted down the gravel road toward his house. He hadn't possessed Jassy's body yet, but he was certain he'd filed a claim on her heart.

And having her heart was more important than having her body alone, he realized with surprise and only a touch of his usual wariness.

THE RAIN CONTINUED throughout the night. Exhausted emotionally and physically, Jassy went to bed soon after Seth left and fell asleep almost immediately.

Her sleep wasn't peaceful.

She tossed and turned, dreaming of Dieter, her parents and the past. Finally she awoke around four in the morning, tense and wide-eyed, going over and over the disclosures she'd made to Seth.

How could she have told a virtual stranger so much? How could she have carried on so, then tried to drag him into her bed to make herself feel better? Her behavior was downright embarrassing! And no matter what Seth had said about her being brave, he'd insulted her, treating her as if she were some fragile china doll in danger of breaking.

Even worse, Seth had indicated she was a coward at heart, someone who ran away from commitment.

A coward! Jassy sat straight up in bed. No matter what Seth had influenced her to say, Jasmin Reed didn't run away from anything or anyone!

She merely moved on whenever she took the notion because that's how she preferred to live her life. She didn't need or want commitment. She'd seen enough broken promises already, thank you very much.

When Dieter had joined the marines, she'd looked for someone else with whom to share her secrets. She'd gotten engaged to the young man she'd been dating, but he'd chosen a career in the air force over a civilian job and marriage to her. They'd parted badly, and Jassy had bitterly chalked up another victory for the armed forces.

Commitment was only a permanent-sounding word. Jassy had seen enough proof of that. Older and a whole lot wiser now, she was more realistic about life. She'd settle for a little understanding and a few laughs. Not that The Wolfman was much for laughing. And not that he understood her, especially not if he thought that weak, crying woman last night was the real Jassy.

Perhaps weakness appealed to Seth. Maybe that's why he'd suggested she should establish a steady, long-term relationship with him.

Well, she'd simply have to straighten him out, and the sooner the better. She didn't need anyone. She didn't need a territory. Or roots. Or relationships.

Tomorrow they'd have a talk.

8

BY MORNING, the sky was clear and sun poured through the skylight, awakening Seth. Smiling, he stretched and reached for a warm body, then realized he'd only been dreaming that Jassy was by his side. His smile faded.

And yet his hopes rode high.

He was certain he and Jassy would be together soon—body, heart and soul. Feeling optimistic, he got up, fixed himself some coffee, and packed for Seattle. He was confident that the members of the Mountain Wilderness Society would be enthusiastic about the lectures he'd prepared.

Then he phoned the vet and went to the cabin to talk to Ben about Snowbird's and the other wolves' injuries. It was midmorning by the time he got to the pens. Jassy and the interns were already busy feeding the animals.

Dressed in an orange T-shirt, with a matching ribbon in her hair, Jassy appeared bright and colorful, as usual. Standing outside the fence, she kept her face toward the enclosure as Seth approached. Her nose wrinkled as the pack tore into a side of beef.

"Morning, Jassy."

She glanced over her shoulder. "Morning."

He searched her expression for warmth, for the new level of understanding they'd reached, and was disappointed when she turned away again. He wondered if she was embarrassed.

"How's Natane?" she asked.

"She's doing well after the transfusion and stitches. Charlie said we'll be able to bring her back in another day or so. Did you check on Snowbird?"

Jassy stared across the enclosure. "Uh-huh. She's depressed."

"A normal reaction. But if you keep paying attention to her, she'll perk up. She likes you."

"I hope I can make a difference for her. Now, if only we could find another pack she could move in with."

"Perhaps a special friend would do."

"A mate, you mean?"

Seth nodded. "Maybe a much younger mate. I can put a pup in with her so she can have the upper paw to begin with. Every wolf, no matter its sex or relationship to pups, feels instinctually bound to raise and take care of them."

"I suppose that'll have to be good enough."

Seth thought Jassy sounded unusually negative. "Are you feeling all right?"

She stretched her lips into a wide smile. "You already asked me that last night. As I told you then, I'm perfectly fine."

But Seth sensed a touch of coldness in her eyes. "And I'm still not sure. You had a hell of a time."

"Well, storms affect people's emotions, too."

Seth knew the storm and the wolf fight had merely triggered feelings that she'd kept hidden for a long time.

"All that electricity in the air got on my nerves," Jassy went on.

"You don't have to make excuses. You already know what I think."

"Sure. I certainly am aware of what *you* think."

He raised his eyebrows. "Do you have something else you want to talk about?"

"Uh-huh." Jassy glanced around, sighting Erin a few yards away. "But I'd rather we had privacy."

Wondering if she'd come to a decision about them, he suggested, "Why don't you walk me back to my house?" He needed to get on the road soon. "I have to pick up my bag and my notes." And maybe he'd get a chance to kiss some of the tension out of her.

"Right, you're leaving for that meeting in Seattle."

"I'll only be gone two days," Seth said as they passed the observation tower and headed down the road.

"Is there some hurry to come back?" When he looked at her questioningly, Jassy amended, "I mean, Ben and the interns will make sure the wolves are taken care of. You could probably use a little vacation."

"Maybe." But why was she suggesting he take days off?

She lengthened her stride, bouncing along as she turned her face up to the sun. "Every day is like a vacation when you travel from place to place, you know. You ought to try it sometime."

He didn't like her tone, which was too bright. Forced. "And what's that supposed to mean?"

"You told me that I need to settle down in one place. I'm telling you that you need to travel. We merely have different ways of looking at life."

Now he was starting to get the picture—one he didn't like. "That's not what we said last night."

"That's not what *you* said. I'm not sure what I did or said. I wasn't thinking straight. Otherwise I would never have let you imply that I'm a coward."

"A coward? Where did that come from?" he growled.

"You said I run away from my feelings," Jassy pointed out. "That's not true at all. I simply don't dwell on the negative ones. It's a conscious choice on my part."

Okay, if that's what she wanted to think. Seth knew she was skirting the issue. "I didn't call you a coward."

"Well, I'm not. I like my wandering life-style. I'd be bored if I had to stay in one place all my life."

He scowled. "How can you be sure of that, since you've never lived in one place long enough to find out?"

"I stayed in Ohio with Mom for a year and a half."

"Not long enough."

She tossed her head. "And who made you such an expert?"

"I'm not going to argue with you." Especially when it was obvious to him she was on the defensive. He also had the sinking feeling that the remark about her lifestyle meant she was rejecting his invitation—that she *didn't want* to get closer—although he wasn't going to make any accusations.

They reached his yard. Hoping for either an end to the nebulous, unpleasant dialogue or a remark he could really sink his teeth into, Seth asked, "Anything else you want to talk about?"

"I just want to reassure you that I will definitely be leaving at the end of August."

"That's what you said when I hired you." Not that he hadn't thought she might change her mind.

"I needed to tell you again—uh, in case somebody starts getting too serious. I've already marked out my route through Idaho—"

"Hold on, here." Seth stopped in his tracks. He didn't like the direction the conversation was taking. "Somebody's getting too serious? Is that 'somebody' supposed to be me?" He *had* been, but he'd also been restraining himself for *her* sake.

She turned to him, her cheeks pink. "I'm not the special sort of woman who knows what a wolf man needs."

"I never said that you were," he told her coldly.

"But Ceil did, and I thought you agreed with her."

"You need to clean out your ears," he retorted.

"You said I needed someone steady, a long-term relationship," she insisted. "It sure sounded like you were referring to yourself."

Seth wouldn't admit she was right for all the tea in China. "You'd better wait for the ring before you tell people we're engaged."

The pink in her cheeks deepened. "So you were only offering your *friendship* last night?"

"That and my bed any time you're ready for a good roll in the hay." Angry, he let his gaze slide over her body.

"Oh, right. When I'm ready...*emotionally*, you mean." She was coldly furious. "After all, you wouldn't want to take advantage of me," she said sarcastically. "Hell will freeze over before I come anywhere near your bed!"

Then she turned and ran just as he should have known she would.

Seth strode in the opposite direction, slamming his front door so hard, the windows in the house vibrated. Grabbing the bag he'd packed and the folder containing his notes, he quickly locked up before climbing into the pickup. In deference to the wolves, he drove slowly past the enclosures but gunned the engine as soon as he was outside the gates.

He sped along the access road and was traveling down the highway before he allowed himself to think of Jassy—another woman for whom he'd mistakenly allowed himself to feel too much, something that hadn't happened often in his life.

The last time had been in graduate school where he'd fallen for another biologist, a woman who'd ultimately rejected his proposal because, she'd said, she hadn't wanted to live in a rural area. If dislike for rural living were the real reason . . .

A teenager who'd always had plenty of dates with the fast girls in high school, Seth had been unable to get to first base with girls from upstanding, respectable families. Not that some hadn't found him attractive.

He'd never forget the devastatingly pretty homecoming queen who'd climbed into his junker one night and wanted to make out—so long as they parked someplace where no one would see them. Smitten, believing he could change Gloria's mind about him if they talked, Seth had agreed. But she'd kept her mouth and hands so busy, he hadn't been able to utter two words.

The next day, Gloria had looked straight through him when they'd passed in the school hall.

That single painful incident had made Seth angrier than all the other times he'd been reminded he was nothing but trash. Availing himself of a bottle of his mother's cheap whiskey, he'd gotten drunk and staged a howling, one-man demonstration on Gloria's lawn. Her outraged, upstanding parents had had him arrested.

Damn! He hadn't thought about that beautiful blonde for years. Nor would he have believed that Jassy, who was a different sort of person entirely, could ever remind him of Gloria—or influence him to act so immaturely.

Because driving like a hot-rodder was definitely adolescent. Glancing at the speedometer, Seth immediately took his foot off the accelerator. He was thirty-five now, not sixteen, for God's sake.

A few minutes later, thinking more calmly, he realized Jassy's reasons for rejecting him had been more complex than Gloria's. Well, she wouldn't have to worry that he'd interfere in her life again. He'd make sure he kept his distance in future.

Ceil's remarks about finding a mate had made him aware of his desire for a partner, someone who could warm him from the inside out and make him feel complete, someone who could assuage the loneliness he'd felt all his life.

And after the tender moments they'd shared the other night, he'd actually thought Jassy might be that woman.

Well, forget it. Whatever *her* reasons, Jassy would be running away again at the end of summer. And to protect himself, Seth had to remember that every moment they were together.

"GEE, I THOUGHT Dr. Heller was only going to be gone for two days," remarked Erin on Wednesday afternoon. She sipped some water from a thermos and gazed up at the tree branches above her. She and Jassy had sat down in the shade to take a break from building the fence.

"Maybe something came up in Seattle," Jassy suggested, wondering if the disagreeable conversation she'd had with Seth on Sunday had anything to do with his extended absence.

"Did he go over his itinerary with you?"

"No, why should he?"

Erin shrugged. "I don't know. You seem to be on real friendly terms with him."

"We're not that friendly, believe me." Jassy didn't want her to get the wrong idea.

Unfortunately, she and Seth would probably never be real friends. He'd been angry and cold on Sunday; she'd been hurt and insulted, yet aware that she'd put him on the defensive. Despite his denial, Seth *must* have started taking their relationship seriously. Or else he thought she was rejecting him altogether.

Jassy wished there was some way she could feel better about the situation. But to do that, she'd also have to be able to ignore her own annoying attraction to Seth. No matter how she tried, she couldn't get her mind off the man.

"There's the truck coming up the road," Erin announced pointing down the hill.

Jassy leaned forward eagerly, expecting to see Seth's pickup. But it was only the Metcalfs' van. Fay waved as she parked by the veterinary building.

Erin scrambled to her feet. "Oops, I forgot Fay was coming by. Can you help me get those wolves over there for her?"

"Sure." Jassy was willing to give Erin a hand. Keith had a class that afternoon, and Ben had gone to town.

Big Bad, Snowbird and the three other injured females were to get additional antibiotic shots that afternoon. Natane, who'd been returned to the refuge on Tuesday, was locked in a large cage near the building and would also have to be examined.

"Boy, I wish Dr. Heller was here," Erin muttered when they'd gotten inside the enclosure. They'd separated the injured and the healthy into two different pens, and now had to run down a playful, rambunctious Big Bad. "Nobody else can handle this guy when he's in this kind of mood."

"We'll get him," Jassy assured her.

"Let's try to corner him one more time."

"Better yet, let's seduce him," suggested Jassy, remembering the chocolate bar she had in her pocket. "He's such a pig." She pulled out the candy, took a bite and smacked her lips. "Yum! Come here, Big Bad, have some." She approached the wolf and held up her arm, while nodding to Erin. "Just keep the collar ready."

Big Bad immediately flung himself on Jassy's arm, daintily taking the chocolate bar from her fingers. No mean feat, considering the wolf's jaws could crush moose bones. While Big Bad was distracted, Erin slipped the choke collar over his muzzle and tightened it around his neck. The wolf coughed as if he couldn't get his breath.

"Isn't that too tight?" asked Jassy, concerned.

"Naw, he's playacting."

Strong choke-collars were necessary for controlling the wolves; the combination of chain and leather would tighten if the animal tried to pull away.

Still, Jassy watched Big Bad closely for a moment to make sure he was okay. Satisfied, she fastened a heavy chain to the collar and wrapped part of the length around her arm. Erin had another wolf ready, so they opened the gate and took the wolves out together.

"This isn't exactly like walking a dog, is it?" Erin laughed when her wolf tried to veer away and she had to jerk the animal back.

Jassy agreed. "They'd need a lot more training."

Big Bad wasn't pulling at his leash but he kept leaning against her, forcing her to walk crookedly. They were halfway to the veterinary building when he started coughing and making choking sounds again.

Jassy stopped, examining the wolf worriedly. "This collar is too tight. He can't breathe!"

Erin, who was several paces in front, called over her shoulder, "Don't do anything until we get inside the building."

But Jassy had already loosened the collar and was trying to adjust it. As she struggled to place her fingers inside the wide leather band, Big Bad squirmed and danced and finally slid his head free.

Free!

Human and wolf stared at each other for a split second; Jassy was too surprised to make a sound. And then

Big Bad took off like a shot, running down the road as fast as his legs could carry him.

"No!" Jassy shouted helplessly. "Stop him!"

"Oh, my God!" But Erin had her own wolf to handle and couldn't help.

"Big Bad!" Jassy yelled as she ran. "Come back!"

But the wolf wasn't listening. Muzzle into the wind, he sprinted for freedom. Jassy ran pell-mell down the road after him. "Big Bad!"

The wolf passed the gatehouse and galloped straight for the open territory beyond. Jassy kept after him, but she was losing the race.

"Big Bad...please!" she cried as the animal shot through the gates, veered to the side and disappeared into a thick copse of firs. Out of breath, she collapsed against a gatepost, her heart pounding. "Big Bad! Come here, boy.... I'll give you more candy!"

But the only answer was the sound of the wind and fluttering leaves. No wolf poked his head out of the underbrush. As soon as the stitch in her side subsided, Jassy began to search the immediate area, calling Big Bad's name and praying he hadn't gone far.

Which was like looking for a needle in a haystack.

Erin finally came out to tell Jassy to take a rest from the search. They might as well wait until Ben or Seth returned and ask them what to do next.

Already distraught, Jassy didn't look forward to Seth's reaction when he learned the escape had been her fault.

JASSY PATROLLED the perimeters of the refuge that evening while Ben drove into Minal to notify the authorities, to ask various friends to keep an eye out for the animal, and to check the outskirts of town himself. Ben had taken the news quietly, hadn't even given her a hard time. And Ceil had been supportive, assuring Jassy the wolf would probably come home on his own. Jassy had appreciated Ceil's kindness.

She didn't think Seth would take the news quite so well and only hoped they could find Big Bad before Seth returned. She had dragged a deer's haunch out to an open grassy area several yards inside the entrance in hopes that the young wolf might get hungry enough to be lured back inside.

Jassy paused near the gates when she heard a low rumble in the distance. It was the roar of an engine, and the beams of headlights soon arced through the trees. Seth's pickup came into sight.

Not wanting him to see her until she was sure she had a grip on herself, Jassy quickly stepped back to hide in the shadow of a large tree. She tried to calm herself enough to figure out exactly how she was going to break the bad news.

The truck slowed as Seth drove through the gates, then turned up the short drive that led to the A-frame, the building closest to the outer fence. Seth parked, got out and looked around. He even glanced toward Jassy's hiding place several yards away, as though instinct told him he wasn't alone. He turned to the back of the pickup and unloaded his suitcase and some packages.

Steeling herself, knowing she had to face him sometime, Jassy decided it might as well be now.

"Seth!" she called, coming out into the open. She didn't want him hearing about Big Bad from someone else. Her palms sweating, she strode toward him. "Wait a minute, I want to talk to you."

He barely glanced her way. "Again?"

She winced. He definitely sounded prickly.

"It's not personal," she assured him so that he wouldn't get the wrong idea based on their last conversation. "We've had a problem with one of the wolves."

He let his suitcase drop to the ground. Unsmiling, Seth waited until she came within a few feet of him.

"So what's going on?"

"Big Bad is loose," she explained, rubbing her damp hands on her jeans. "He managed to escape on the way to the veterinary building this afternoon."

"How the hell did that happen?"

His harsh tone made the blood drain from her face. "It was my fault. I was adjusting his collar."

Seth frowned. "You loosened the collar enough to let him get away?"

"I—I thought he was choking." She licked her lips nervously. "He squirmed out of the collar before I realized he was putting on an act."

"And then you let him run right off the grounds?"

"I couldn't catch—"

"Great!" Seth cut in. "And now he'll be shot or trapped by some insane zealot who hates wolves."

Though she'd expected him to be angry, his words made Jassy flinch. She hadn't wanted to think about Big Bad's fate if they didn't find him. She clenched her shaking hands into fists. Though she couldn't be sorrier, she'd be damned if she would grovel for Seth's forgiveness.

"I didn't do it on purpose," she said tersely. "And we are trying to find him. Keith and Erin are coming back and we're going to keep an all-night watch. Meanwhile, Ben is asking the sheriff and his friends in Minal to keep an eye out for Big Bad."

"And you know what that's going to do?" Seth challenged, looming over her so that Jassy stepped back. "That's going to alert anyone in Minal who owns a gun that it's open season on a marauding wolf."

"Big Bad? He might maraud a chocolate bar," Jassy said, thinking of the way she'd lured him earlier. "But he'll probably starve if someone doesn't feed him."

"But people around here won't believe that. Why do you think a recovery program is so difficult to put in place?" he demanded, coming closer. "People are afraid. They think wolves will kill their livestock, or the game that hunters want for themselves. Parents will be hysterical about the safety of their children. By morning, there'll be dozens of men out with rifles." His face was only a few inches from hers when he added, "Big

Bad is so innocent and trusting, he'll probably walk right up to one of those jerks and get his head blown off."

Jassy caught her breath and steadied herself with a hand against the pickup. "Maybe not. Ben thinks he'll head for the wilderness area, maybe find his way up into the mountains."

Seth gazed directly into her eyes. "If you couldn't handle a simple task, why didn't you say so and let someone else do it? You've always got to prove you can do anything, don't you? Putting yourself in danger is one thing. But this time, you've sentenced an innocent animal to a certain death."

Swallowing hard, Jassy felt tears pricking the backs of her eyelids. Seth turned away. If he hadn't been two days late returning to the refuge, she wouldn't have been handling Big Bad in the first place. She thought of telling him so, but she knew that would only anger him further. Besides, laying the blame on someone else wouldn't change what had happened. She watched Seth pace the area and stare out into the forest as if his night vision were equal to that of his charges.

"Big Bad won't be killed if I can help it!" she swore softly.

"I don't know how you think you can stop the inevitable." Seth sounded resigned.

"I'll get flashlights and go out and search the surrounding area on foot." Jassy only hoped she would be able to recognize wolf tracks when she saw them.

"All by yourself?" Turning toward her, he shook his head. "That's the most ridiculous thing I've ever heard. For one, you'd be wasting your time setting out in the dark."

"Then I'll wait until daybreak."

Seth spoke more to himself than he did to her. "With all the upheaval in the pack happening the other day, Big Bad very likely took off to find a new territory somewhere in the wilderness. Maybe he will head for the mountains."

Jassy took another deep breath. "I can be ready at dawn."

"Forget it. I'm going alone."

"Two pairs of eyes are better than one," she insisted. "Ben and Ceil aren't as quick as they used to be and the interns are in the middle of a study they've been working on for weeks. That leaves me, so I'm going."

"Only if I say so."

"I'm going even if you don't say so—"

"You'll just be in the way. I work better alone."

"You'd do everything alone if you could, I'm sure," Jassy retorted, her temper flaring. "That way, you wouldn't have to deal with other people. Well, this time, you'd better get used to the idea of having help, because I'm coming with you. And if you try to leave me behind, I'll just follow you."

Seth's eyes narrowed. "It's rough country out there. Thick forest, steep inclines."

"I can handle it. I took a mountain-climbing course at a college in New Mexico."

"We'll have to carry heavy backpacks with sleeping bags, food, and maybe a tent."

"I have my own sleeping bag and backpack."

"We might have to stay out several days and nights."

"I know how to camp. I'm coming with you, Seth. You're not going to discourage me."

Seth's jaw tightened. "Be ready at daybreak, then. You'd better not slow me down, and you'd better be good."

Or what? Jassy's triumph at getting her way was marred by Seth's threatening tone. He wasn't bothering to hide his hostility. She brooded about the source of that hostility as she returned to her trailer. There was no doubt he hadn't been able to forget their last argument any more than she had.

What a mess! If she didn't feel so responsible for Big Bad, she wouldn't have insisted on going anywhere with him. She certainly wasn't looking forward to entering the deep dark forest with The Wolfman.

9

"YOU KNOW, THIS REMINDS me of a rain forest in Japan," Jassy said as she followed Seth into the dense growth of the valley that paralleled the twists and turns of the nearby Quinault River.

Seth had given Jassy no quarter in their trek into the wilderness. Picking up Big Bad's trail outside the refuge at daybreak, he'd tracked the wolf first to Big Creek and then to the river valley. They'd been going strong for more than six hours now and were in the heart of the rain forest. If he'd really believed Jassy would slow him down, he was wrong. Even carrying a loaded backpack, she kept up without complaint. He had to admit she was a real trooper.

And as if she'd forgotten they had fought, she kept a conversation going despite his determination to maintain a distance between them.

"I like all kinds of forests," she was saying. "The Black Forest of Germany is one of my favorites."

Never having been off the continent himself, Seth merely grunted. He kept a sharp eye out for places where Big Bad's large paws had crushed the delicate mosses and plants such as trillium and oxalis, which cushioned the forest floor beneath their feet.

To be truthful, as angry as he'd been with Jassy the night before, Seth was grateful for her company. He'd called himself every kind of a fool for thinking about her at all, but he'd missed her while he'd been in Seattle. Work that usually absorbed him had barely kept his attention. He'd purposely stayed away the extra days to try to prove that he could do without her.

He'd only missed her more.

Undeterred by his silence, Jassy said, "Actually, I prefer wilderness areas of any kind to big cities."

Something else they had in common—not that she would want to hear about it, Seth thought grimly.

"The mountains of Spain," she murmured wistfully. "The deserts of Africa . . ."

So what if he'd missed her, Seth reflected. She didn't want any kind of relationship. Jassy had allowed herself to get carried away physically with him one night, then had refused to associate with him the next day. Just like Gloria, the prom queen.

In a sunny clearing, Seth paused to check several sets of clear tracks in a patch of bare earth. He bent and inspected a dropping.

"Wolf scat. Pretty fresh. Big Bad can't be too far ahead of us."

"So we're catching up to him?" Jassy asked hopefully.

"We're not losing him," was all Seth would say.

After than, Jassy fell silent until Seth finally called a halt just after noon.

"Lunch."

They stripped off their backpacks and he could see how uncomfortable Jassy was. In the cloying dampness of the rain forest, strands of hair that had pulled free of her French braid stuck to her cheeks and neck. As she rolled her shoulders, her breasts stood out in damp relief against her fire-engine-red T-shirt. He tore his gaze from the tempting sight and noticed her wince as she arched her back. Yet she made no complaint. She dug into her gear, found the paper sack that Ceil had prepared, and threw him a sandwich and an apple.

"Thanks."

"I'll be right back."

Jassy walked into the trees, undoubtedly to take care of personal needs.

Seth sat at one end of a fallen tree from whose rotting trunk a tiny row of seedlings sprouted. Over the next few years, their roots would straddle the nurse log, seeking the mineral-rich soil below. Eventually the log would decompose and a whole row of young trees would be left on stiltlike roots. Seth bit into his sandwich, thinking of the power the rain forest had to fascinate him.

When Jassy returned, she found a place for herself on the log, as far away from him as possible.

Feeling a little guilty that he'd driven her so hard all morning, he tried to be civil. "Have you spent much time in the wilderness?" he asked.

"Off and on." She studied the sandwich she was unwrapping. "I have to make enough money to live. Often that means taking a job in a city."

"Do you have any particular skills or do you just wing it like you've been doing the past few weeks?" When she glared at him, he added, "That wasn't a criticism. Actually, you've been doing a helluva job, Jassy. I, uh, shouldn't have gotten on your case the way I did about Big Bad. He could have given the slip to anyone who didn't know his little tricks."

Her eyes widened as if in surprise. "Are you actually apologizing?"

"Yeah, I guess I am. Thinking about losing Big Bad to some hunter's rifle or to someone prejudiced by all the negative stereotyping . . . Well, it got me down. I shouldn't have taken my frustration out on you."

"It was my fault, though," she admitted. "Erin told me to wait until I got inside before fooling with the collar."

Jassy was silent and thoughtful as she ate. This time the lull in conversation was more comfortable, and Seth realized how stressed he had been for the past several days. He'd missed having Jassy's natural warmth to brighten his day, to make him smile, to make him feel human.

He just plain *needed* Jassy, and he didn't know what the hell he was going to do about it.

Finishing her sandwich, she bunched the wrapping into a tight little ball and cleared her throat.

"I want to apologize for what happened before you left for Seattle," she said. "I took what happened the other night too seriously. I overreacted and maybe imagined some things...." She peered at him as though trying to gauge *his* reaction. "Well, I'm sorry."

Suddenly discomfited, not wanting to rehash the argument, Seth changed the subject. "So, tell me about your adventures in the big cities of the world."

Jassy seemed relieved, as if she, too, welcomed the lighter topic. "They weren't all that exciting, trust me. I'd visited most of the major European cities and a few in the Middle East and Africa before I was sixteen. So when I set out on my own, I tried to avoid big cities. Still, I couldn't always manage it. I waitressed in New York for a couple of weeks, changed oil and did lube jobs on cars in Omaha for more than a month. And I cleaned up cages in a Santa Barbara pet store all last winter."

"So that's where you developed your affinity with animals."

"I've always liked animals," she said, "even though I never had the opportunity to be around them much in the past."

"Didn't you have pets when you were a kid?"

She shook her head. "Different countries have different entry and quarantine regulations about bringing animals in and out. My father insisted that I could always leave a pet behind and get a new one at the next base, but I didn't think that would be fair to the animals, so I never had any. What about you? Have you always liked furry creatures?"

"They don't put qualifications on friendship," Seth said. *Not like the people in Minal.*

She stared at him thoughtfully, then asked, "How did you start working for Ben?"

"He found me. I was doing time for petty theft and vandalism by washing the police cars and the fire engine every day. The only reason I didn't go to reform school was because my mother and the chief were good friends." Seth hated to think just how many men in the town had been "good friends" with his mother. "Anyway, Ben needed help at Wolf's Lair and he believed he could teach some juvenile delinquents about responsibility through taking care of the wolves."

"You."

"He talked the chief into placing me in his hands. I couldn't have been happier. I'd always been fascinated by animals. I figured I'd have one up on all those kids who thought their little dogs were hot stuff. I wasn't quite ready for the wolves, though. They were as hard to handle as I was. But I learned to respect and love them."

"And Ben and Ceil."

Seth nodded. "They didn't take backtalk from the wolves or from a whelp like me, and they both have big hearts. It wasn't long before they treated me like a son— I guess because they didn't have kids of their own."

"And because you proved yourself worthy of their love," Jassy added.

Seth shifted uncomfortably. He'd never been good at talking about feelings. He stood and stuffed his litter and hers into the paper sack and shoved it into his backpack. He'd always respected the forest, even as a rebellious teenager.

"Take a couple of minutes to stretch or whatever," he said. "Then we'd better get going if we want to catch up to Big Bad before dark."

When they set off a few minutes later, Jassy was glad to get going again. The conversation had been getting too personal, and she wanted to keep her emotions on an even keel. As it was, she felt much better than she had for days. Seth obviously couldn't hold a grudge any more than she could.

While their reason for the hike into the wilderness was serious, Jassy took pleasure from her surroundings as they spent hour after hour traversing the valley. Almost junglelike in its luxuriant growth, the rain forest was dominated by Sitka spruce and western hemlock. Some of the evergreens stood more than three hundred feet high. Big-leaf maples were so heavily draped with moss they were nearly camouflaged. Trailing shrubs tangled with licorice and sword ferns, which sometimes sprang up out of the tree trunks high above her head. And every so often, Jassy would glimpse a ray of sunshine and a splash of color amid the pervading green—the pink of bedstraw or the yellow of the pioneer violet.

She was relieved that Seth was no longer giving her the silent treatment. With harmony restored, they traveled well together, keeping each other company while looking for Big Bad. As they trekked farther away from civilization, it was invariably Seth who spotted wolf signs. He even pointed out a place where Big Bad probably had taken a midday snooze.

Jassy saw black-tailed deer feeding on leaves, and who only looked up placidly at the humans' approach to confirm they were unthreatening. Squirrels chased each other along a Sitka spruce branch, one jumping to an adjoining hemlock, the other sitting up and chattering its annoyance. The forest was also home to black bear and cougars, neither of which she hoped to see.

Eventually they came to an intersection of sorts, meeting a wide trail cut through the dense forest.

"An elk trail," Seth said, inspecting the crushed undergrowth carefully. "Roosevelt elk crisscross the national park, going from one water source to another. Here, look," he said, pointing to a print that was different from the others. "Big Bad must have been thirsty."

"And hungry," Jassy said.

"Let's hope he doesn't recognize elk as food. Considering how inexperienced he is at catching his own dinner and their substantial size—"

"He'd get himself hurt," Jassy finished, her guilt renewed.

For more than two hours they followed the elk trail, which ended at another creek. Big Bad's tracks led them right up to the bank. Seth checked to make sure the wolf hadn't backtracked.

"He must have crossed the creek," he said, leading the way across the channel of calf-deep rushing water. On the other side, he searched the ground carefully. "But he didn't come out here."

"You don't think he got swept off his feet by the current?" Jassy asked, feeling renewed worry and exhaustion setting in.

"Possibly. More likely, he was playing in the water and came out somewhere downstream."

Jassy spotted a pair of river otters, and farther on, a beaver poked its nose from the thick growth along the bank. But there was no sign of Big Bad.

"Maybe we should each take one side of the river and—"

"In the morning," Seth told her. "Sun's down. It'll get dark fast in the woods."

Worried that they hadn't caught up to Big Bad yet, Jassy was glad for the rest. She was exhausted and her feet and lower legs were uncomfortably wet and cold despite the mild evening.

"Where do you want to make camp?" she asked.

Seth looked around. "Over there." He pointed to an area where the trees had been thinned by a recent storm.

"Perfect. Near fresh water. Lots of down timber. And we'll be able to see the night sky if we make a shelter under that giant log over there."

He led the way to the fallen tree that was wedged over an incline, leaving a gap of several feet between it and the ground.

"What about the tent you brought?" she asked.

"I like being in more direct contact with nature. The tent would protect us against rain—not that much of it gets through these trees. The growth seems to absorb the moisture before it can hit the ground." He stopped and slipped off his backpack. "But if you want to use the tent—"

"No," Jassy said quickly.

Though agreeing might have been the wiser choice.

She already knew she couldn't trust herself around Seth now that her anger—her only defense—had dissipated. Even thin nylon walls between them would have been better than nothing. She could have used some protection. Lying next to him, lulled by the sights and sounds of nature . . . who knew what could happen?

Nevertheless she shed her backpack and said, "A natural shelter sounds great."

"Why don't you strip branches from that tree," he said. "It's a recent fall. We can use the boughs to make a canopy and a bed. The needles still look pretty fresh. They'll make a good cushion under our sleeping bags."

Seth pulled an ax and a portable shovel from his backpack frame. The shovel's scoop was hinged flat against its handle. He snapped the scoop in place and began digging on the incline, widening the opening between log and earth. Jassy took the ax to remove the branches.

A quarter of an hour later, they had a cozy shelter. The emerald green of the forest had deepened to a dark jade in the fading light. Next, Seth dug a fire pit while Jassy chopped some firewood. Within a short time, bright golden-red flames lent a cheery glow to their camp. Placing her sleeping bag over some extra fir boughs, Jassy made a sitting area in front of the fire.

"Ah." Sighing, she sank to the ground. She removed her boots and socks, carefully placing them near the fire to dry. Wiggling her toes, she turned them toward the fire. "Oh, to have dry feet again." Jassy sank back lengthwise on her sleeping bag and let her eyelids drift closed. "You're a real woodsman," she said, appreciating the level of skill he'd shown. "I'm a rank amateur by comparison."

She punctuated the statement with a loud yawn, but couldn't muster the strength to be embarrassed about it. She was used to hard physical work, but she couldn't remember when she'd felt so fatigued.

"But you have potential," Seth told her. "I used to spend a lot of time alone in the forest when I was a kid. You learn by doing. Shelter. Water. Food. Everything you need to live is available if you know where to look and how to use what you find. I used to think about living in the wilderness. No one to bother me or make demands."

Sleepily aware of his words, Jassy murmured, "But you would never do that if it meant abandoning your wolves." She'd just recognized a major difference between them: Seth could survive without civilization, while she manipulated civilization in order to survive. "Would you?"

"No. Hungry?"

"Mmm." She turned onto her side and, drawing her knees up to her chest, curled into a tight little ball. Lying there felt so good. The crackle of the fire lulled her, its warmth enveloped her body. "But I'm too pooped to find the food just now. Give me a little while—"

"No problem. I'll get dinner."

She opened her eyes to see Seth bending over his backpack, which he'd dragged near the fire pit. He pulled out a small pot and a packet of food.

"Wait a few minutes and I'll help," she murmured as her eyelids fluttered closed.

Seth stopped what he was doing to watch Jassy as sleep claimed her. The flames threw flickering ribbons of gold and red over her face and neck. She sighed and the sound vibrated through him like a caress. She looked so warm and inviting, he had to fight the urge to forget about food and climb onto the sleeping bag with her.

He could imagine her outrage if he did.

He dumped the freeze-dried stew into the pot. Try as he might, Seth couldn't stop himself from creating fantasies. The setting was romantic—dark woods, a star-studded night sky, a waning moon, a crackling fire. And his body responded to the soft, lovely woman nearby.

Seth added water to the stew, setting the pot on a log at the edge of the firepit far enough from the flames so the contents would heat slowly.

He glanced at the curled-up form on the sleeping bag and knew there could be no other woman for him while Jassy Reed was around. Her leaving at the end of the summer wouldn't guarantee he could forget her, either; fool that he was, he'd fallen in love with her.

Why did he always choose the wrong woman? he wondered. Was it some kind of curse? Did he need to stake a claim on someone totally unsuitable just to challenge himself?

But Jassy wasn't the wrong woman and she wasn't unsuitable. Maybe he was giving himself too hard a time, as usual. Jassy was like the creatures of the forest he loved so much: a little wild, wanting freedom, yet responsive to a gentle touch.

He dominated the wolves, so why hadn't he dominated her, forced her to respond to his will?

Because he didn't want to dominate her. She wasn't a wolf. She was a woman. She had to want him of her own free will. But he could help her will along a little, Seth decided. He knew what he had to do. If he could make Jassy see that she belonged at Wolf's Lair with him, win her over, then she wouldn't think of leaving. Not at the end of the summer. Not ever.

What if he couldn't convince her to stay? What if she didn't want him when he had his heart set on her?

He was going to drive himself crazy if he didn't stop thinking in circles like this. Rising, he gathered up his sleeping bag and set it in the shelter. Then he chopped enough wood to keep the fire going all night with some to spare for breakfast. He stirred the stew. The aromatic fragrance made his stomach tighten. He hadn't realized how hungry he was. If Jassy didn't waken soon, he would be tempted to eat it all himself.

Then again, offering food was an effective method of taming a wild creature, Seth reflected, smiling. He sat on the edge of Jassy's sleeping bag and held the pot near her nose.

"Mmm, smell," he murmured, waving the rising steam toward her. "Stew's ready."

She stirred and passed the back of a hand over her face.

"Aren't you hungry?" he asked.

"Mmm-hmm." Her eyes fluttered open. "I'm starving." She yawned. "Was I asleep?"

Seth couldn't resist teasing her. "You were snoring."

"I don't snore," she protested, sitting up and yawning again. "Do I?"

Laughing, he stirred the stew and tasted it. "This is pretty good," he said. "You probably woke all the animals in the forest."

Her eyes narrowed. "It's too early for them to be sleeping."

"Have some." He held the spoon a few inches from her mouth.

As suspiciously as any other creature in the forest, she sniffed, then delicately took a bite. "That's delicious."

"Amazing what they can put in little foil packets these days," Seth said, taking another spoonful himself.

"Amazing what a thirty-mile hike can do for an appetite," she returned.

"I don't think we hiked quite that far."

"Could have fooled me. Say, don't you have another spoon somewhere?"

"Yep."

But rather than looking for it, he offered his own once more. Jassy stared at him for a moment, a myriad of emotions flickering across her features. Seth was sure she was about to search for the second spoon herself. Surprising him, she quickly ate the stew in his spoon.

Jassy drew back, and Seth saw a wariness in her expression that hadn't been there before. Had she figured out what he was up to? If so, she wasn't skittering away like a frightened doe. She stood her ground, moving closer to him as they shared the stew.

Seth couldn't control his body's arousal at her nearness. As she leaned closer to eat more stew, he imagined touching her warmth. His jeans tightened uncomfortably.

"Your turn," she said, when he forgot to scoop another spoonful.

He did so clumsily and splashed sauce on his hand. Holding his gaze, Jassy slid her fingers around his wrist and brought it to her mouth, and licked the back of his hand with her tongue.

Seth's pulse raced. Was she issuing an invitation . . . ?

Heat crept up Jassy's neck even before she let go of Seth's hand. Something elemental was occurring between them and she didn't have the power or the desire to stop it. It was inevitable, she told herself. She'd only been fooling herself to think otherwise. From the moment he'd appeared out of the quiet forest, she'd known The Wolfman would one day overpower her with his intensity.

He devoured her now with his eyes, yet he made no move. He sat still, as silent and as patient as his charges in the refuge.

Jassy could hardly breathe.

When Seth put down the half-empty pot, giving up the pretense of eating, she was immediately on edge. Unspoken desire hung between them. And yet still he made no move.

I can wait. . . . You can set the pace. His words came back to haunt her. Was he waiting for her, just as the alpha male waited for the signal of the alpha female?

Her hand reached toward his face, seemingly of its own volition. She stroked his beard then slid her fingers through his shoulder-length hair and loosened the tie that held it back. Her heart was beating with such force, she swore Seth could feel the pulse in her fingertips as she stroked the taut cords of his neck.

"My emotions are under control tonight," she murmured, though her chest felt as if it were being squeezed by a vise.

"Are they?"

"I mean, I know what I'm doing."

"What *are* you doing?" he asked. His words seemed forced.

Seth was as nervous as she! Jassy giggled. He frowned. She moved closer and smoothed the ridges on his forehead with her lips. Any reservations she'd had seemed to melt away. Closing her eyes, she kissed a trail down his nose, across his cheek and along his beard, stopping only when she found his waiting mouth.

Seth didn't wait any longer. With a smooth lunge, he pinned her to the sleeping bag.

Lying on her back, she pulled at his shirt as his lips ground into hers. He removed her T-shirt and bra, then ducked his head to catch a nipple between his teeth. She gasped at the sensation. She wanted to lie back and simply let Seth do what he would, but she undid his shirt buttons, belt buckle and zipper.

Reaching into his briefs she found him, hot and heavy and ready for her. A thrill of arousal shot through her. She explored farther and Seth jumped. With a hiss through clenched teeth, he removed her hand and rolled onto his side to strip off his clothing. As she did the same, he pulled a wallet from his jeans pocket.

"What . . . ?"

"Shh," he whispered, slipping something out before tossing the wallet aside.

He'd brought protection. Jassy didn't know whether to be relieved or angry. Had he *assumed* he was going to bed her? Reviewing how this situation had come about—at her instigation—she didn't think he'd assumed anything.

But then, when Seth rubbed his beard along her inner thighs and nipped at her sensitive flesh, she couldn't think at all. She lay back and tangled her fingers in his hair. He worked his magic, caressing, kissing, laving, nipping, finding the very heart of her desire and arousing her to a degree she hadn't thought possible. His tongue flicked and probed. She writhed and called out his name, begging him to stop, to enter her fully.

He ignored her pleas and continued his torment until Jassy cried out in ecstasy. Then he plunged deep inside her. She clutched his shoulders, ran her hands down the muscles of his chest as he stroked her with a thrilling hardness, using his hands and lips and the rhythm he set to force her to new heights.

"I love you, Jassy," Seth whispered, gently biting her ear, than her lips.

She urged him on with her hands, with the thrust of her hips. "And I love you."

Jassy hadn't known it until that very moment, when they reached fulfillment together, and Seth cried out, his shout wild and wolflike.

But as they calmed and lay quietly together, Jassy began to feel apprehensive. *What now?* she wondered.

"*A-a-w-w-oo-o-h* . . .

Both Jassy and Seth stiffened. He stared out into the forest.

"Seth, you don't think that's—"

"Could be. I don't see who else would be out here howling." Cupping his mouth with his hands, he tilted his face toward the sky and returned the greeting. "*A-a-w-w-oo-o-o* . . ."

There was silence, then another heartrending howl.

"It is," Jassy cried, recognizing the young wolf's distinctive sound. "It's Big Bad!"

"Maybe we can guide him to us."

As Seth called again, Jassy scrambled into her clothes. Then, she, too, joined the chorus. After a few minutes, however, the wolf's howl grew more and more faint.

"He's going in the wrong direction. Why would he do that?" Jassy asked. "Do you think he wants to be alone out here?"

Seth scowled as he dressed. "No. He's got to be scared and ready for a friendly pat and some easy food by now. For some reason, he can't get to us."

"A-a-w-w-oo-o-o . . ."

The faint howl then faded to nothing.

Jassy stared into the silent night, feeling the young wolf's loneliness as if it were her own. And why not? Making love with Seth had brought her one step closer to being trapped by her own feelings.

10

SETH WAS NEITHER stupid nor insensitive. He knew Jassy wasn't totally happy about their having made love, even if they did zip their sleeping bags together and spend the night in each other's arms.

When they rose before dawn the next morning, she seemed to be distancing herself from him. As usual, she kept her feelings to herself, and Seth didn't have time to wheedle them out of her. He had a wolf to find.

They were on the move as the first rays of light crept through the Sitkas. Seth crossed the creek to cover the opposite bank, leaving Jassy to follow along that side. They headed downstream, each carefully checking for signs of Big Bad.

Seth picked up Big Bad's trail about a half hour later.

"It looks as if he went farther downstream and back-tracked this far," he yelled, noting the multitude of prints, as if the wolf had been pacing back and forth. "I think Big Bad was right here last night, but he couldn't figure out how to get to us."

The creek was wide and the bank was too steep to negotiate for at least a hundred yards in either direction. The wolf would have been anxious and confused.

"Maybe he's nearby," Jassy said, raising her voice over the rush of the current.

"Yeah, but now we have to find a place to get you across."

They found it farther downstream where the creek narrowed and spilled over onto low banks. Several rocks jutted up out of the water, and Jassy used them as stepping-stones to keep her feet dry. By the time they returned to the spot where Seth had picked up the wolf's prints, they'd lost nearly a half hour.

Determined to catch up with the wolf as soon as possible, Seth drove himself harder than normal and hoped Jassy could keep up. Big Bad had to have slept, so he might not be too far ahead of them. The wolf had crossed some virgin territory and his were the only tracks to be found. When they came to another cross-roads meeting a wider, more definite trail, Seth let out a sound that was a mixture of relief and disgust.

"What is it?" Jassy asked.

"He's traveling west. Backtracking."

"Heading for home?"

"He doesn't know where home is, or he would have been there in time for dinner last night. He's just wandering."

"Let's hope we can get him home for dinner to-night."

"What's the matter?" Seth asked, his gaze steady. "You don't want any more stew?"

Jassy flushed and fell silent. Seth had guessed she would, when reminded of what had happened after dinner the night before. Sighing, he started out of the clearing. They trekked at an even more rapid pace for several hours, stopping only for a few minutes' respite at a time. But by half past one, Seth knew he couldn't go on much longer without food.

"Yell when you see a place you'd like to stop," he told Jassy. "I don't know about you, but I'm starving."

"We can stop here if you—"

Several high-pitched screams interrupted her.

"Big Bad!" they said in unison—then took off running down the trail. They could hear a woman's strident voice.

"Get out of here, you beast! Children run!"

Seth cursed. "No! Don't run!" he yelled at the top of his lungs. "Stay where you are and he won't hurt you!"

"Mommy, he's eating our lunch," a young girl cried.

"We have to get out of here or he'll eat one of us next," the mother responded. She sounded angry and scared.

Seth and Jassy crashed into the clearing. Big Bad was standing on a plaid blanket, finishing off what looked like a whole roasted chicken."

"Big Bad!" Jassy cried.

The wolf barely glanced up at her before polishing off the last of the carcass. Next, he started on a container of potato salad. Seth reached him first and caught him by the scruff of the neck. Big Bad whined and immediately rolled onto his back. He looked a bit ridiculous with mayonnaise all over his muzzle.

"Is that creature yours?" the red-haired woman demanded, standing several yards away from the wolf, hugging two carrot-topped little girls to her sides. They were probably campers who'd taken a hike to enjoy their lunch away from the nearby campground.

"Yeah, he's mine," Seth said, relieved that she had listened to his warning and stayed put. He released his backpack and retrieved a collar and leash. "There's no reason to panic and set a bad example for your kids."

"Who are you?" She was furious. "I should have you arrested for endangering my children. You can't just let a wolf go anywhere he wants."

"Right, I set a wolf free so he could find his own lunch," he muttered.

"It's not his fault," Jassy explained quickly as Seth slipped the collar around the wolf's neck. "The wolf got away from *me* by accident the other day. We've been tracking him since daybreak yesterday morning."

"Oh, my God, I should have brought the rifle with me!" the woman cried.

"That's the kind of attitude that eradicated wolves from most of this country," Seth responded angrily, paying no attention to Jassy when she put her hand on his shoulder. "This guy is half tame. If he were really wild, like he should be, he wouldn't have come within a mile of you."

"You're from that Wolf's Lair place, aren't you?" the redhead asked. "My husband told me we'd have trouble with you wolf lovers someday, even though we live in Pineville. No one on the Peninsula is safe."

Seth's temper was about to explode by the time she'd finished. "Now, that's a damn stupid—"

"We're real sorry for your fright," Jassy interrupted diplomatically, attacking Seth's shoulder with her fingernails. "But believe me, Big Bad was probably more scared than you. He was hungry because he doesn't even know how to get his own food."

"Well, he seems to have done a pretty good job of it. He ate ours . . . and ruined our day!"

"I'd be happy to reimburse you—"

"Never mind. Just get that monster out of here."

"He doesn't look like a monster, Mommy," the younger girl said. "He looks like a doggy."

The woman clutched the children to her more tightly as if she was afraid they might run up to the "doggy" to pet him. Seth shook his head in disgust at the prejudice she was passing on to her girls. He handed Jassy the leash while he hefted his backpack into place.

"I really do apologize," Jassy said again. "You were in no danger. Are you sure we can't compensate you for the food?"

"No, just go. Please."

Taking the leash, Seth didn't waste any time leaving the picnic site. She could start trouble for the refuge, and he knew it.

Big Bad trotted easily between them, alternately leaning into Seth, then Jassy. Though he managed to clean his muzzle on their jeans, he didn't try his choking trick on them. No doubt he'd had enough freedom to last him a long time.

About ten minutes down the trail, Seth figured they'd gone far enough.

"Let's have lunch over there," he suggested, moving into a dense area of the forest. "We don't want to give that woman another heart attack if she brings her kids by here and happens to see us while we eat."

He made sure Big Bad's leash was secured to a stake in the ground. The wolf whined, seemingly disappointed that he'd be separated from the humans. Lying down and placing his muzzle between his paws, he stared at them with soulful yellow eyes.

"We've got trail mix and fresh fruit," Jassy said, removing them from her backpack. "Unless you want to build a campfire and make something more substantial."

"I want to get home as soon as possible." Seth sat with his back to a moss-covered maple. "The trail mix and fruit will be fine."

Disappointed at the dim-witted way he'd handled the sticky situation with the woman, Jassy threw him an apple and a sealed plastic bag filled with dried fruits, nuts and seeds. Seth could be so kind and caring when he wanted to be, but he could also be a pain in the rear.

"Why did you tell the woman not to run?" she asked. She'd ease her way into the real issue.

"Big Bad is so playful he might have thought it was a game. And if one of those kids fell . . ."

Jassy was horrified. "You don't think Big Bad would have hurt them?"

"Anything can happen when you're dealing with a half-tame animal. They have certain wild instincts that don't vanish merely because they've been hand-raised. I told you before, you can never trust a wolf completely—no more than you can trust any other undomesticated animal. No matter how funny or charming he seems to be, Big Bad is no doggy."

Jassy was silent as they ate. She was still trying to figure out how best to give Seth a piece of her mind. Maybe the direct approach would be most effective.

"So, what was the purpose of giving that woman a hard time?" she asked.

"That woman was acting out of prejudice and stupidity!"

"No more so than you. She was afraid for her children, Seth, and from what you just told me, rightly so. You didn't even consider her feelings. Do you have compassion only for animals? What about human beings?"

Seth had the good grace to look ashamed. "All right, maybe I was out of line. But worrying about Big Bad being shot had my gut tied up in knots. Then, when she started in about her rifle, I lost it."

"You didn't lose it only with her," Jassy stated flatly. "The way you dealt with her is the way you handle anyone who doesn't work on the refuge. When it comes to outsiders, you have a chip on your shoulder a mile wide."

"I have my reasons—"

"Everyone has reasons to be unhappy," she cut in. Didn't she know it! "Some of us do the best we can to change the situation and don't take it out on other people."

"Right. You pick up and leave instead of dealing with relationships and problems."

He was accusing her of running away again, of being a coward, Jassy thought, biting hard into her apple. He was trying to take the heat off himself. But she wasn't about to let him get away with it."

"Why can't you admit you have a bad attitude? Maybe then you can do something to change."

"Maybe I don't want to change."

"At least that's honest, if not admirable."

He scowled at her. "People in Minal treated me and my mother and my sisters like dirt when I was growing up. They considered us trash and couldn't even make an effort to be decent to us."

"Did you ever give them a reason to?" she probed. "The townspeople mightn't have been fair to you, but you aren't helping any by being cold and belligerent. Honestly, you would think Wolf's Lair was your personal territory to defend with tooth and claw."

"If I don't, who will? Ben and Ceil have done their share, God knows, but they deserve a little peace of mind now. That means I have to take on the fight."

Fight. Why did people think that warfare of any kind—even a cold war—was a reasonable course of action? Seth's attitude was another reason for Jassy not to get any more involved with him than she already had.

"Someone has to bend, to be the voice of reason," she said.

"And why should it be me?" Seth demanded.

"You're better educated than anyone in town. You had to have brains to get your doctorate. Why don't you use your intelligence on something other than the wolves?" Jassy asked. "Or use it *for* them. Until you make your peace with the townspeople, you won't see any change in their attitude about the recovery program."

Seth didn't deny that. He didn't respond at all. Taking her cue from the stubborn man, Jassy dropped the subject and quickly finished her lunch. She didn't know why she'd gotten herself so worked up over his predicament in the first place. The wolves weren't *her* problem.

She would leave them, along with everyone else at Wolf's Lair, at the end of the summer.

THE SUN HAD SET before they reached the refuge, where the others were all waiting for them. Keith and Erin took care of Big Bad, Ceil fixed Jassy and Seth a hot

meal and Ben called the authorities to let them know the crisis was over.

They'd barely eaten and given the older couple an edited version of their trek through the wilderness when Jassy's eyelids began to droop. Excusing herself, she refused Seth's offer to walk her to her trailer and was thankful when he didn't insist. Exhausted as she was, she didn't have the strength to handle him.

She also told herself that a good night's sleep would do wonders for her sense of purpose.

But when Jassy awoke at daybreak, Seth was her first thought. She was more confused than ever. She struggled through her chores, thankful that he was nowhere in sight. The bright spot of her morning was spending a few minutes with Snowbird, whose enthusiasm for human companionship always made Jassy smile.

When Ceil suggested that she take the afternoon off and come for a drive with her, Jassy readily agreed. The time had come to free the raccoons Ceil had hand-raised.

"I thought we'd take the road to the campground," she said, loading the two carriers into the back of her station wagon. "Then we can walk them in a mile or so before letting them go." She slid behind the wheel and Jassy took her place in the passenger seat. "Ironic, isn't it?" she asked with a sigh. "Yesterday, you and Seth find Big Bad and bring him home from the wilderness and now we're going to set my babies free out there."

Jassy heard the catch in the other woman's voice. "Sounds like you don't want to."

Ceil started the engine and pulled away from the cabin. "What I want and what's right are two different things. Charlie and Cynthia were born free. Circumstances dictated that a human had to give them a hand for a while, but now they're old enough to take care of themselves—I hope."

"I'm surprised you don't set them loose near the cabin," Jassy said. "Then you could see them once in a while, make sure they were okay."

"That would be terribly selfish of me. And they would never learn to do for themselves. Worse, they might wander down to the wolf enclosures...."

Jassy hadn't thought of that. Wanting to cheer up the older woman, she forced a smile to her lips and said, "I'm sure they'll miss you, but they'll do fine on their own."

Ceil headed the station wagon onto the unpaved road that would take them a half-dozen miles into the wilderness. They drove along in companionable silence for a few minutes, but Jassy sensed that Ceil had something on her mind.

"Seth was out of sorts after you left for your trailer last night," Ceil stated a short while later. "Anything happen out in the wilderness that you want to talk about?"

Jassy started to deny there was any problem, then hesitated. Maybe talking to good-hearted, practical Ceil would give her some perspective.

"We, uh, discovered that we care about each other."

Ceil laughed. "About time. I knew it all along."

"But I *don't want* to care," Jassy protested.

"Nonsense."

"No, really. When I leave at the end of the summer—"

"Then don't leave," Ceil said. "No one wants to see you go, especially Seth. He more than cares about you. That boy's head over heels in love."

And so was she—not that Jassy wanted to explore the depths of her feelings. "He'll get over it."

"I'm not so sure about that. Seth's had to get over more than his fair share in his life. He was dealt a tough hand, which only made him even tougher. His trust has always been hard-won." Ceil clucked. "I don't know if that boy'll ever get over another major disappointment."

Sorry that she'd given in to the temptation to discuss her relationship with Seth, Jassy mumbled, "You're exaggerating."

"I don't know how much he told you about himself—"

"I know that he was a juvenile delinquent and that Ben straightened him out. He also told me people in Minal think of him and his family as white trash."

"He lost his daddy to a sawmill accident when he was eight. His mama turned to the bottle, poor woman. Hard to blame her, losing her husband, with three small mouths to feed and having no education or skills. Mary did her best, but it wasn't good enough. Drink became her only comfort." Ceil hesitated, then sounded uncomfortable when she added, "Drink and the men who soothed her loneliness and helped her take care of her kids financially."

Jassy swallowed hard.

"Seth started getting himself into trouble soon after his daddy died. You can imagine how people treated him. His reputation was worse than he deserved. And when he was in high school, a nice girl wouldn't look at him twice—not in public, anyhow. He didn't have a decent relationship with a girl until he was in graduate school."

"What happened?"

"Said she didn't want to live in a rural area, but I think the folks in Minal had something to do with changing her mind about him."

"Then she couldn't have loved him!" Jassy insisted hotly. "Or she would have made up her own mind about Seth."

Anger at such prejudice and injustice coursed through her. Seth might have his faults—he was without doubt the most stubborn, determined man she'd ever met—but he was also the most wonderful.

"Seth has come a world away from that unhappy boy Ben rescued from washing police cars," Ceil went on. "Once he developed a sense of responsibility, he stopped getting into trouble and earned good grades. Ben did what he could to help Seth with college money—every penny of which the boy has made good, by the way—and Seth did what he had to do to get an education. He applied for scholarships, grants, loans, and he took every crummy job you could think of. But once Seth Heller makes up his mind to do something, he doesn't just flap his jaws, as Ben would say. He does it."

"And he decided he wanted to carry on Ben's life-work," Jassy stated.

"He wants to further Ben's dream with one of his own, the recovery program. Seth doesn't believe wild creatures belong in pens any more than I do. Ben doesn't agree with him. Thinks it'll only cause trouble in the long run—maybe get a bunch more wolves shot. They go around and around about it, but neither of them will budge an inch."

How many people would sacrifice their lives to a cause that not only kept them poor, Jassy wondered, but made them outcasts from society as well?

The things she was learning about Seth's background gave her a different outlook on her own. She'd always had difficulty getting along with her parents, but she'd never wanted for material things. Education was something she had taken for granted and, in some ways, wasted. And, as mistaken as they were about what was right for her, her parents had wanted her happiness.

A lump formed in her throat as she thought that her leaving might well break Seth's heart. But she would make him understand before the time came. As Ceil said, Seth didn't believe wild creatures belonged in pens. She would make him see that she, too, needed her freedom.

Ceil pulled her station wagon over to the side of the road. "This is as far as we go. I hope you're up to a little more walking."

"I'll manage."

She and Ceil each took a carrier and set off on the nearby hiking trail that led straight toward the mountains. Jassy was so preoccupied with thoughts of Seth that she hardly saw the natural beauty around her. A couple of miles along, Ceil called a halt near a bend in the creek that wound near the trail.

"Looks like a good place," she said. "There's plenty of shelter and water and food."

Ceil knelt and opened the carriers, then pulled something from her pockets.

"Come on out of there, you rascals." The raccoons came straight to her and took the treats from her hand. She petted them, then pointed them in the direction of the underbrush. "Now, skedaddle. Go explore your new home."

Watching the raccoons, Jassy was saddened. The two animals seemed confused—excited by the new sights and sounds, but not entirely sure that they wanted to leave Ceil. Not unlike her own feelings when it came to leaving Seth.

Jassy decided that she would make every minute she stayed count. She would enjoy her relationship with Seth, make the most of it for the rest of the summer, while convincing him that her going away wouldn't mean she loved him any less. Like his wild charges, she, too, needed freedom.

Jassy didn't have the faintest idea where she wanted to go. For once, she couldn't summon up her normal enthusiasm for a new adventure, but she told herself it was because she was still wrapped up in the one at Wolf's Lair. Once she was on the road again, she'd be back to her usual self.

For some reason, however, the highways that normally beckoned in her mind's eye suddenly appeared deserted and uninviting.

11

"Hɪ, Iʀᴍᴀ," Jassy said as the preceded Seth into the local grocery store that afternoon.

"Jassy."

Sitting behind the checkout counter, Irma Rudolph nodded politely. Then she turned her usual frozen expression on Seth. His instant reaction was hostility, but he forced himself not to let it show. Nodding curtly, he picked up a wire basket and headed for the canned-goods aisle.

"How's business?" Jassy asked, clearly in no hurry to get her shopping done.

"Same as always. Slow."

"Maybe things will pick up soon."

That was Jassy, Seth thought, grabbing a can of string beans and another of whole tomatoes. Always positive. She'd given him a lecture after they'd found Big Bad. Someone had to bend, she'd said, obviously meaning him. But Irma Rudolph had held him in such contempt for so many years, he wasn't sure he wanted to change things.

"I'm thinking about giving this place up for good," Irma said as Jassy worked her way down the other aisle.

"My back's been acting up again. And sitting around most of the day gives me more misery."

Having to carry cartons of heavy goods into the storeroom wouldn't help, either, Seth thought as he added potatoes and an onion to his basket. He saw a stack of them next to the door and remembered Irma's complaining the first time he'd brought Jassy in for groceries.

"You should get one of those special lumbar cushions," Jassy said. "I hear they're great for people who sit a lot. Takes the stress off your back."

"Lumbar cushion? Hmm."

"You'd probably have to go to Pineville to get one," Jassy went on. "Or maybe the pharmacist here could order one for you from a supply catalog."

"I think I'll talk to Ralph about it. Thanks for the suggestion."

In all the years, Seth had never heard Irma thank anyone for anything. But then he'd never paid much attention to the woman who'd always been unpleasant to him, and he'd certainly never tried to be nice to her. Thoughtfully, he pulled a package of chuck steak from the small meat freezer. It was important to Jassy that he try to mend the past with the inhabitants of Minal, and because she was important to him, he decided to try.

"That'll be twelve dollars and forty-three cents," Irma said stiffly when she totaled his purchases.

Seth gave her fifteen and, as she counted out the change, indicated the pile of cartons on the other side of the door. "Say, you wouldn't need some help getting those boxes into the back, would you?" he asked gruffly.

The store owner gave him a suspicious look. "You know a kid who needs some spending money?"

"No, not offhand." Actually, he didn't know any of the kids in town anymore. "But I could move them for you if you'd like."

Her eyes narrowed further. "Why would you want to do that?"

So much for bending. Ready to get the hell out of there, Seth took his change and slipped the two single bills into his wallet, the coins into his pocket.

"I just thought I might save your back some strain."

"If you're serious," Irma said slowly, "I would appreciate your help."

He was aware of Jassy staring at him with amazement as he replied, "I'm serious."

Irma rose stiffly and led the way through the store to the back room where she pointed out a two-wheeled dolly.

Seth had the cartons moved in three quick trips. And when he returned to the counter to get his groceries, Jassy was waiting for him with a dazzling smile. Irma smiled at him, too, for the first time in all the years he'd known her. Jassy might have been correct about his being as guilty as the townspeople when it came to keeping up bad relations. He couldn't believe what a small act of kindness had accomplished.

"Thank you, Seth," Irma said as he picked up his bag. "Have a nice evening."

"You, too."

As they left the store together, Seth realized that Jassy's influence was something he could handle on a permanent basis. He'd be happy to tell her so now that she'd gotten over the rotten mood she'd been in after rescuing Big Bad. When she'd left the Laskys' cabin and had refused to let him walk her to her trailer the night before, he'd been afraid she wanted nothing more to do with him. He hadn't gotten much sleep, worrying about it. But Jassy had dispelled that awful notion when she'd returned with Ceil.

Thank goodness.

"That was really nice of you," Jassy said as they set the groceries in the back of the pickup. "I knew you could win Irma over if you tried."

"I did it for you, not for her."

"Whatever the reason, you made her see you in a different light, and I'm glad."

"And what kind of light do you see me in?" he asked.

Before he could figure out what she was up to, Jassy stood on her toes, smacked a kiss on his cheek and danced out of his reach before he could grab her. All he caught was an armful of air and her enticing scent. She climbed into the passenger side of the truck and he hurried to slide behind the wheel.

"At the moment," she finally said, sinking down into the seat, "I see you in a very favorable light."

"Good. Then you'll have dinner with me."

"I'd love to. Where do you want to go?"

"My place for stew."

The atmosphere in the pickup suddenly became charged. Without taking his gaze from her happy smile, he started the engine. Her smile faded, to be replaced by a very serious expression.

"Seth, I've been doing some thinking . . . about us."

"What about us?" he asked cautiously, pulling out of the parking lot.

"I want to make the most of every minute we can spend together."

He grinned with relief. "Sounds good to me." Better than he could have hoped for.

"I want to have great memories of—"

"'Memories'?" he cut in.

"Yes. When I leave." Jassy sounded a bit nervous when she added, "At the end of the summer. I did tell you I would be moving on then."

But he'd been foolish enough to think things had changed. Seth jammed his foot on the accelerator and peeled rubber. What had happened to her vow of love?

"After what's happened between us, how can you think of leaving?" he demanded.

"Seth, it's not that I don't love you. I do. You have to believe that."

"You love me but you're going to leave me. Just like that."

"Not just like that. A big part of me wants to be near you. But I wasn't meant to stay in one place any more than the wolves you love. We're different, you and I. You're a man of the earth and I'm a nomad without roots. I need to be free to roam. I want memories to take with me . . . but if you're set on something more permanent . . . then I guess I'm not the right woman for you."

Not the right woman? Feeling as if he'd been kicked in the gut, Seth practically hit the ceiling. "Why don't you let me decide that?" he shouted.

"I don't want you to fool yourself."

"Is that what you think? That I'm a fool for wanting more than a fling?"

She shifted uneasily. "No, of course not."

"Sounds like it to me," Seth said with disbelief, thinking Jassy was going to drive him crazy if she kept this up. "You love me, but my returning that love makes me a fool because you're not going to stick around to see how it all turns out."

Jassy let out a frustrated sigh. *Now what?* she wondered. She was only trying to be honest so that Seth wouldn't be operating under any false impressions. She was certain that she'd taken the right tack by telling him the truth—so why didn't she feel better about it?

They drove in angry silence until they approached the Wolf's Lair sign on the highway.

"What the hell?" Seth slammed on the brakes and pulled the truck over to the shoulder.

Jassy's eyes widened. Someone had pinned up a picture of a wolf and used spray paint to draw a circle around it with a line slashed through it.

"'No Wolves In Washington,'" she read aloud. "A warning?"

"Some of the locals must be trying to give us a message," Seth muttered. "No doubt they're still worrying about the new enclosure. And maybe they heard about Big Bad scaring the woman and her kids."

Jassy recognized both anger and worry in Seth's tone and knew that he was afraid the antiwolf people wouldn't stop at signs. What terrible timing! They were turning on him just when he was starting to make an effort to get along with them. He'd gone out of his way to be kind to Irma. The problem, a difficulty much larger than her own troubles, drew her closer to the man she loved. Wanting to comfort Seth, she reached out and covered his hand on the steering wheel.

"Let's go make that stew," she suggested. "We can clean up this sign in the morning."

He gave her a curt nod, pulled the truck back onto the highway and turned down the side road. A few minutes later, they drove past his place toward her trailer so she could put her groceries away. Jassy tried not to think about anything but the present, but as they passed the wolves and she gazed toward the area that would soon be the new enclosure, she was reminded of her own torment.

Was any limitation, no matter how generous, really freedom? Or would the big enclosure be an illusion, just as her staying on at the refuge would be? Again Jassy thought of the raccoons. Though Ceil had raised Charlie and Cynthia, they had willingly headed into the unknown rather than stay within reach of her loving hands. And no matter how loving Seth was, Jassy would feel trapped if she did as he expected.

He stopped the pickup in front of her trailer.

"I'll only be a minute," she assured him. "Should I bring anything?"

"You're all I want," he said.

Those simple, heartfelt words echoed through her mind as she entered the trailer and put her milk and cheese in the refrigerator. She stalled for a few minutes, trying for a more positive attitude, but she could still hear the words when she climbed back into the truck.

Not that Seth said anything further.

Jassy would have preferred an argument rather than the silence that had her on edge by the time they pulled up in front of his A-frame. She kept expecting Seth to start on her again. He surprised her, though. While he was obviously still upset, he was trying to hide the fact.

"I thought I'd make you the real thing tonight," Seth told her as they entered his kitchen area. When she looked at him questioningly, he explained, "The stew."

"Do you have a food fixation or something?"

"Not really." He stared at her a moment before saying, "What we had the other night was nice, but I wanted to show you how good it could be when done right."

Jassy got the distinct impression he wasn't talking about food. Her heartbeat accelerated. "You made dinner the last time," she said as if he were. "Shouldn't I return the favor?"

"You can help. Working together is bound to bring two people closer."

That statement made her feel inexplicably guilty. Determined not to show as much, she put on her brightest smile. "You're the chef. Tell me what to do."

"Help me wash these vegetables and cut them up."

It wasn't long before the awkwardness between them faded, to be replaced by a different kind of tension. Jassy couldn't stop imagining the two of them upstairs in his loft. Their view of the sky would be quite different from the one they'd shared the other night, but it wouldn't be any less beautiful.

And their making love again wouldn't be any less thrilling—a fact she couldn't stop thinking about, especially since Seth took every opportunity to touch her, to tease her, all the while pretending to concentrate on the meal preparation.

"Excuse me," he said. Reaching for a couple of potatoes, he slid against her back and let his breath trail over her neck.

Savoring the goose bumps that made her shiver, Jassy couldn't resist joining in the game. "No problem," she responded, leaning over for a clean knife and purposely brushing her breast against his forearm in the process.

He stepped back and critically watched her cut a potato. "You could do that more efficiently."

He moved in behind her, placing his hand over hers. He proceeded to demonstrate, guiding her hand in a chopping motion, and using enough body talk to take Jassy's breath away.

When he stopped, she let the knife drop and arched back against him. She tried to memorize the feel of his hard male form. He caught her hips and forced them against his. Tipping her head back against his shoulder, he raised her arms, slid her palms over his beard and threaded her fingers through his hair, loosening it from its ponytail.

Meanwhile, his hands created delicious sensations as they caressed her breasts. Her eyelids fluttered closed. "I can feel your heartbeat," he whispered, gently kneading the soft flesh.

"And I can feel yours," she returned, aware of the pounding pulse against her back.

Jassy tried to turn in his arms, but Seth made a sound of protest and pinned her to him. Undoing the buttons of her shirt and unzipping her jeans, he opened her to his more intimate touch. As his callused hands explored all her tender, secret places, Jassy felt as if she were overflowing inside. All thought fled. She'd never felt such wild desire.

Even so, in a last attempt to salvage the lighter mood they'd created with their game, she gasped out, "I thought you were hungry."

He wasn't buying, though he growled, "I am," in her ear. He then brushed his beard across the sensitive skin at the back of her neck and bit the tender flesh hard enough to make her gasp with arousal. "Starving."

Wanting to concentrate on Jassy, to eradicate any barriers between them, Seth lifted her in his arms. Before she could protest, he found her mouth, stilling any objections, and carried her up the loft stairs. He wasn't playing now; he had a mission and was deadly serious.

But, although she was seduced, Jassy was still playing. Laughing softly, she unbuttoned his shirt, teased his lips with her tongue and pressed her breasts against his chest.

By the time Seth had taken the last step and entered his sleeping area, he couldn't wait to take her nipples in his mouth and suckle them while he made love to her. Though reluctant to free her for even a moment, he let her down.

Flipping a switch, he threw the loft into semidarkness. Seeming as mesmerized as he, Jassy was stripping, dropping her clothes into a pile at her feet. Quickly, he did the same.

But when Seth reached for Jassy, she flashed him a grin, slid from his grasp and, laughing, tried to get away from him. She didn't get far. He caught her near the bed and pushed her gently onto the mattress. She tried to scramble across the bed on her knees.

Before she could get halfway to the other side, Seth leaned over, grabbed her around her waist and nibbled at the back of her neck. Her laughter stopped as she sucked in her breath and a sound of pure pleasure escaped her. Seth knelt on the bed directly behind her, her back against his chest, her buttocks against his hips, her knees between his.

Jassy leaned back against him, turning her head to kiss him. Seth had access to all the soft, feminine places he'd been longing to explore. He tasted her earlobe and kissed her throat where her pulse beat strongly. He trailed his fingers over her collarbone and shoulders, pressing his open palms against her breasts and caressing them with his fingers. Then he caught her nipples between his forefingers and thumbs.

Jassy gasped with satisfaction, arching to press herself against the length of his body. She reached back with both hands to stroke his arms, his sides.

Snaking one hand down her stomach and through silky hair, Seth found her damp and ready, and opened her to his touch. He caressed her with his fingers and slowly probed deeper, all the while playing on her neck and ears and the soft flesh of her shoulders with his lips and teeth and tongue. Jassy moaned and writhed, moving her buttocks against his throbbing groin. He leaned forward, supporting her weight until she rested her elbows and forearms on the bed.

"Now, Seth," she urged. "Now!"

She guided him as he entered her. Holding her hips to set their rhythm, he plunged deeper, then slowly withdrew so that only his tip was inside her. She gasped and he plunged again. Sensation flooded him as he moved. He wanted to seduce Jassy totally, to bind her to him emotionally, to *make* her love him as he did her.

With one hand, he stroked her inner thigh and worked his way slowly to her center. His fingers met moist flesh and he matched the rhythm of his hand to that of his lower body. Small cries escaped her throat as she rocked her hips, inciting him, yet Seth held back, even when she tensed and arched against him in release.

He slowed the rhythm until she rested her forehead on the mattress.

"Seth," Jassy whispered, trying to turn around. "Let me touch you, pleasure you the way you did me."

But he kept her gently in place. "Not yet."

Then he started moving again, this time with more urgency, touching her breasts, her stomach, everyplace possible, seducing her in every way he knew. He felt the tension building in her yet again, even as she seduced him.

Breathing heavily, Jassy reached through the arch of her thighs to find him. And at her insistent touch, Seth was lost. A growl rumbled in his chest as he climaxed, the sensation heightened when Jassy did the same, this time with a wild cry.

Seth moved to lie on his side, taking Jassy with him. She turned so they were face-to-face. He cradled her against his chest, never wanting to let go, and she held on to him as if she felt the same.

"I love you, Jassy."

"And I love you."

But something about the tone of her voice put Seth on edge. He felt as if he was losing her already. Determined to bind her to him, to make her commit herself, he stroked her hair, then slid his hand down her spine.

"You see how good it can be when two people are meant for each other," he murmured seductively.

Jassy stirred in his arms and adjusted her position, creating a slight space between them. Clearly she was trying to avoid the topic.

Seth grew more desperate. "Things change, Jassy, when we least expect it. And people can change if they want to. You told me that. I wasn't convinced, but I tried. And look what happened—Irma was pleasant to me. So you were right all along. You should feel great about that. I took the first step and I promise I won't stop there, no matter how difficult it might get for me, if only you'll do the same."

She pulled out of his arms without meeting his eyes. "I should be going."

"We haven't had dinner yet," he said, though he wasn't interested in eating. She needed an excuse to keep her there until he could get through to her.

"I'm not very hungry."

When Jassy tried to scoot off the bed, Seth gripped her arm, effectively stopping her. "You're running away again. Why?"

"I'm not running anywhere," she insisted. "I have things to do."

"What's more important than us?"

Her expression closed, Jassy jerked her arm free and slid off the bed.

"Come on, Seth, give me a break. Making love was wonderful. You're wonderful. We're wonderful together. I admit all of that, okay? But don't try to force me into making promises that I can't keep."

He threw his long legs over the edge of the bed and watched her dress. "You can keep promises if you want to."

"You believe the wolves should be free. Why not me?"

"The wolves deserve freedom, but not to be alone or without a home. Most wolves travel in packs and every pack has a territory. To them, that's home."

Jassy finished buttoning her shirt. "The universe is my home—"

"A lone wolf really is a sorry sight," Seth cut in, his anger rising. He was tempted to tell her she was full of bull, but he knew that would only alienate her. "A loner's always on the fringe of things. Never loving, always feeling left out, as if he's missing something wonderful. That's how I felt until you came into my life. I can't believe that's what you want, Jassy."

"Then you don't know me as well as you think you do."

"I know you as well as I need to," he assured her. "You're scared and that's all right—"

"There you go again." She glared at him. "I don't have to listen to this!"

"If you care about me at all, you will!"

"I do care, but that's not enough for you."

"How can it be enough when you won't agree to give us a chance? Every time I think about your deserting me I feel empty inside." Anger, hot and unreasoning, prompted him to shout, "I might as well be in love with some illusion, for all the good my relationship with you is doing me! You want to be as free as a will-o'-the-wisp—here one minute, gone the next. What do you think your moving on is going to do to my life? I'll be worse off than if I'd never met you!"

She gave him a stricken look and Seth knew she had misunderstood. Before he could say anything else, she was flying across the room and down the stairs.

He jumped up and leaned over the railing. "Jassy, wait. I didn't mean that the way it sounded," he called, but she didn't bother to look up as she sped toward the front door. "Jassy!"

Then she was gone, escaping to her trailer.

"Damn!"

Going after her immediately might make things worse. Seth sank to the bed, hoping against hope that she wouldn't stray even farther away....

12

SHE WAS NOT A COWARD, Jassy assured herself as she strode across the refuge grounds. And Seth had a lot of nerve implying that she was, merely because she enjoyed leading a nomadic life-style. She was used to moving from place to place, seeing the world, stopping when it took her fancy.

She'd never really known anything else.

But how to convince Seth of that? She was in such emotional turmoil, she could hardly think straight. And why should she want to convince him of anything?

He'd just about said he wished he'd never met her.

She felt incredibly hurt even as she knew that wasn't what he'd really meant.

More anxious to leave than ever after this latest go-round, Jassy wondered if she ought to do just that. She'd been planning to wait until the end of summer, but she could take off sooner. Leaving Seth would be difficult at any time. Arguing about her plans every time she saw him would be more than she could bear.

When she got to the trailer, Jassy decided she would pack her things, then take off at first light. And that didn't make her a coward!

As she passed the enclosures, she sensed the wild pack was restless. The skitter of paws hitting the earth caught her attention. Stopping, she took a good look around. Wenutu, one of the wild males, was circling the enclosure close to the fencing.

Something was definitely wrong.

Her eyes automatically swept to the small holding pen. The waning moon silvered the area.

Empty!

"Snowbird?"

Jassy ran closer. No wolf. She checked the gate. Locked up tight. How could Snowbird have disappeared? Then she saw fresh earth mounded next to the fence and realized what had happened: Snowbird had dug her way into the wild pack's enclosure.

"Oh, my God, they'll kill her!"

Trying not to panic, Jassy was about to go for a fire extinguisher when she heard footsteps coming from the direction of Seth's place. Thank God he'd come after her! Her resentment fading in light of the new crisis, she turned toward the sound.

But it was Ben, not Seth, who approached.

"We have a problem!" she said urgently. "Snowbird—"

"Finally found herself a home," Ben finished for her.

"What?"

She whipped around and scanned the wild pack's domain. Sure enough, the white wolf stood near the den. Lucifer, the silver-tipped black male who'd reminded her of Seth the first time she'd seen him, was circling Snowbird. He was clearly interested and not in the least hostile.

"I noticed she'd disappeared while you and Seth went for groceries," Ben told her. "Then I spotted her and Leotie going to it."

Jassy turned her gaze to the other side of the pen. Lying near one of the younger wolves, the alpha female of the wild pack rested her muzzle between her paws. If Leotie wasn't going after the intruder...

"Snowbird won a domination ritual?"

"Must've got tired of being beaten up all the time."

"I don't believe it. After all our worrying, Snowbird found the courage she needed to assert herself." Jassy suddenly realized she could no longer identify with the white wolf. Sadness for herself mixed with her joy for Snowbird, confusing her. "Snowbird finally found her place," she said softly, her mind once again churning with her own seemingly unsolvable problems.

"Maybe she got inspired. Lucifer's probably a pretty attractive fella to a female," Ben said. "Maybe Snowbird couldn't resist and decided that she'd do anything to be with him."

Ben's gaze was as direct and piercing as that of another wolf man she knew. Jassy sensed Ben wasn't just talking about the animals.

Swallowing hard, hoping he wouldn't ask, she mumbled, "Have you told Seth about Snowbird?"

"Just now. I, uh, would've told him sooner but the two of you seemed to be occupied."

Jassy's face flamed and she was thankful it was too dark for Ben to tell. How much had he been able to see or hear from the outside? And then she realized that if Seth knew about Snowbird, he'd be arriving to check things out at any moment.

She indicated the wild pack. "Is there anything we should be doing to help the situation?"

"Let nature take its course."

She breathed a sigh of relief. "I'll do that. I was just on my way to the trailer."

"I know."

Another blush embarrassed her further. Ben knew too much. Like the wolves, he didn't miss anything. Backing away, almost saying she'd see him in the morning, Jassy caught herself before she spoke the lie. With a wave, she sprinted away.

She wouldn't be seeing Ben again, she told herself. She wouldn't be seeing any of them. Not Keith or Erin or Ceil or the wolves.

Especially not Seth.

The thought left her empty inside—the same way Seth had said he'd feel if she deserted him. But she told herself her going was for the best.

Still, when she was inside the trailer and determinedly packing her saddlebags, she felt like a traitor. Like a thief sneaking away in the middle of the night after having been entrusted with something precious.

But of course that was nonsense. She'd contributed a lot to Wolf's Lair in the couple of weeks she'd been there—both physically and emotionally. She'd done the chores, taken care of the wolves and put up fencing when no one in town would do so. She'd rescued Snowbird from possible death and had seen the wolf through a tough time. And she'd shown Seth that it was possible to change people's attitudes toward him if only he made the effort.

Change.

Seth wanted her to change, but she was happy as she was, right? No ties. No commitments. But could she leave Wolf's Lair? Or was she lying to herself?

Jassy set her saddlebags by the door. Then she glanced out the window toward the enclosures. Moonlight washed over Seth as he stood there, talking to Ben. Her fingers pressed against the glass as if she could reach out to him one last time. Just seeing the man she loved put her emotions in a state of turmoil.

As if a knife had severed an integral part of her being, Jassy mourned Seth's loss even though she hadn't left the refuge grounds!

Could she do it? The insistent doubt recurred.

"I can do anything I want," she muttered, pulling her hand away from the window. At that moment she wanted to be free to roam as before. But she feared Seth would remain forever in her heart.

After taking a quick shower, Jassy slipped into a thigh-length T-shirt, panties and socks. She braided her hair, moisturized her face and hands. She was ready for bed but didn't feel at all sleepy. Needing something to keep herself busy, to occupy her mind, to dissipate the adrenaline rush that held her wide-eyed and on edge, she pulled out her travel book and began to page through the section on Idaho.

She gave up when she realized she hadn't digested a single word.

That she was planning on going without even saying goodbye preyed on her mind. But how else was she to free herself of the close, trapped feeling that threatened to choke her? She wasn't sure she *could* leave with everyone pulling on her, urging her to stay, telling her that she was needed.

Dumping the book in a saddlebag, Jassy threw herself into her bed. She needed sleep if she was set on a dawn departure. But no matter how hard she tried to relax, she lay wide-awake, torn by something deeper than sadness. Grief filled her—the kind of grief she'd felt for Dieter when she'd learned he'd been killed.

But Seth wasn't dead, Jassy told herself—though he would be to her if she were never to see him again.

How could she turn her back on things that had come to mean so much to her? Why couldn't she take a chance on this place and on the man she loved? Just because she'd spent her whole life on the move didn't mean she couldn't change her life-style.

Change.

The thought of staying at Wolf's Lair—of making for herself a permanent place with Seth in his territory—put Jassy in a panic.

Any time she'd ever allowed herself to care for anything or anyone, that thing or person had been taken from her in one way or another. And that lifelong insecurity had been preventing her from admitting that she needed a home and family, needed a man with whom she could share a new life.

Jassy finally faced the truth: She'd spent her entire adult life running from relationships because she feared they wouldn't last.

She *was* a coward.

That was why she was willing to leave the first place she'd ever lived in that felt like a real home. And the first man who had ever won her heart even while making her face the truth about herself. Everything ended sooner or later—how well she knew that. And she had trouble believing her relationship with Seth would be any different.

But what if she were wrong?

Change.

Did she have the courage?

Jassy stared out at the play of shadow and moonlight on the trailer ceiling. She'd come to the most important crossroads in her life. She was so wrapped in thought she almost missed hearing the crunch of tires on gravel and the sound of an engine.

Afraid that something had gone wrong with the wolves, after all, she got to her knees and crawled over the mattress to look out the window facing the enclosures. The moon was momentarily covered by clouds and she strained to see in the dark. No headlights moved over the road, but she could make out a black bulk against gray shadows cast by the security lights. A truck. The pickup coasted to a stop beneath the trees. At once there was movement in the open back—lots of it. Then she remembered the warning painted over the Wolf's Lair sign.

Heart hammering in her chest, Jassy flew off the bed, pausing only to slip on her boots and grab her cycle keys. By the time she ripped open the door, the moon was sliding out from under its cover. A half-dozen men were jumping down from the back of the truck. Bull was leading them. And her worst fears were realized: They were armed with rifles and obviously meant to shoot wolves!

Whatever it took, she would stop them from slaughtering the defenseless animals. Throwing a bare leg over her motorcycle saddle, Jassy was even more horrified when she spotted Seth moving directly into their path. He was unarmed.

"Bull. Boys. What can I do for you?" Seth asked quietly as he blocked their route to the wolf enclosures.

"You can get out of our way and let us at those wolves, Heller!"

Other voices, some slurred, chimed in. All were in agreement.

Seth knew he had little chance of defeating a half-dozen half-drunk men alone. Ben had gone to bed hours ago, leaving him with his thoughts of Jassy, but that was just as well. Ben tended to be too hotheaded and would have risked getting hurt.

As Seth had learned eons ago, if he could defeat the head bully, the others wouldn't have the nerve to stand up to him. He concentrated on the ruffians' leader.

"I'm not going anywhere." He narrowed his gaze on Bull. "You're the one who's going to get out."

"Don't count on it, Wolfman."

Uneasy, Seth stood his ground. While the others might have been drinking, Bull sounded as if he were cold sober for once. That would make disarming him the more difficult. But he couldn't show the enemy any hesitation.

"You're trespassing on private property," Seth stated against the sudden roar of a motorcycle.

"And what're you gonna do about it?"

Not daring to unlock his gaze long enough to see what the hell Jassy was up to, he said, "I'm going to stop you, Bull!"

The other man barked out a derisive laugh as the bike came closer. "How're you fixin' to do that? You're not armed and there's only one of you."

"Two of us!" Jassy shouted.

"Hey!" a man yelled in reaction as she headed her motorcycle straight through the knot of trespassers.

Bodies scattered behind Bull; a rifle went flying.

"Whaddaya think you're doing?"

"What the hell!" cried another.

While the roughnecks were momentarily distracted, Seth took advantage of it. He grabbed Bull's rifle with both hands and rolled backward to the ground. Bull didn't let go of the weapon and came crashing forward. Seth grunted in pain as Bull's weight hit his chest and the rifle barrel banged against his forehead, making him see stars. With difficulty, he struggled out from under the heavier man. When he wiped one hand across his forehead, his fingers came away bloody.

"Get the girl!" Bull shouted to his buddies.

Distracted by his concern for Jassy, who was having difficulty staying out of the others' reach, Seth didn't see the two men until they were on top of him. Still winded, he couldn't move fast enough. Each grabbed one of his arms. They spun him around toward Bull, whose rifle butt slammed into his side. Seth heard his ribs crack as an awful pain shot through him.

Seth went down. He saw the motorcycle jerked out from under Jassy. Though she went flying and landed hard on her hip, she rolled to her feet and headed straight for the men who'd been holding him.

"Jassy, no!" he warned her.

But she was already slamming a boot toe to the back of one man's knee. Taken off guard, he stumbled forward. Without hesitating, she jumped on his companion and put a stranglehold on his throat. The man went to his knees with her still hanging on.

"Damned she-wolf!" cried Bull. "If a man wants a job done, he has to do it himself."

As if watching slow-motion action, Seth saw Bull's rifle point straight at the woman he loved.

Ignoring his injuries, Seth flew to his feet, lunged forward and crashed into the leader. And with the superhuman strength born of desperation, he wrestled the rifle from Bull's hands and hit the other man across the side of his head. Bull sprawled on the ground and Seth pinned him there by pressing his foot on the beefy man's windpipe.

"Go ahead and move and it'll be the last thing you ever do," Seth warned. "Jassy, are you all right?"

"Great," she said, then, "Oof," as she was knocked to the ground.

Seth was already pointing the rifle at the man who'd just pushed her down. "You can have the first bullet."

He raised his hands and moved away from Jassy, who quickly scrambled to Seth's side.

The remaining men drew together.

"Let's get out of here," muttered one of them.

"You aren't going nowhere, you scumbags!" Ben yelled from a short distance away.

Seth glanced back to see both Ben and Ceil hurrying to join them. Ben had a shotgun. Ceil, a rifle.

"Ben, did you call for help?"

"You betcha. The state police will be here shortly.
And we're gonna press all kinds of charges on these
goldurned rodents. Illegal trespass, assault and bat-
tery, reckless endangerment. Anything we can think
of."

"These sons of bozos are going to be sorry they
stepped foot on our place," Ceil added.

Seth removed his foot from Bull's neck and let him
join the others. He was startled when he realized Jassy
had picked up one of the rifles and was pointing it at the
hoodlums. Before he could say a word, he heard the si-
rens.

The authorities had arrived.

"HOPEFULLY THE UPRIGHT citizens of Minal and other
towns around here will think twice before causing *us*
trouble again," Jassy said as the police cars carted the
offenders away a half hour later.

"Us?" Seth echoed, raising his eyebrows. Crusted
with dried blood, the skin on his forehead twitched.

Jassy wanted to run to him, to throw her arms around
him; but now that the furor was over, she was feeling
awkward and embarrassed about her own involve-
ment in the physical altercation.

Seth turned to Ben. "You and I should call a town
meeting and try to work up some support."

"Won't do no good," Ben predicted.

Seth was looking at Jassy when he said, "You never
know. People can change. It's time I faced those who

still see me as a troublemaker. I can try to convince them that all of us on Wolf's Lair have both the wolves' and *their* best interests at heart."

Gratified by his change of attitude, Jassy was worried about his physical condition. She noticed he was holding his side stiffly. And he flinched when he moved.

"Somebody had better look at those ribs," she said worriedly.

"They just need to be taped."

"You think they're broken?"

"I'd be surprised if they weren't."

Concerned and fighting tears now that the ruckus was over, Jassy said, "We have to get you to a doctor."

"You *both* need to be checked out," Ben said.

Seth frowned as he stared at her scraped leg. "We'll do that as soon as reinforcements arrive."

"Seth!"

Ceil rejoined them. "The boy's stubborn, isn't he?"

She'd gone to call the interns after the men had decided the refuge needed someone on guard at all times until they were sure that things had calmed down.

"Hey, Jassy, Ben and I can stand guard till Erin and Keith get here," Ceil said. "Why don't you take Seth to your place and fix him up real fine."

Hearing the implication in that suggestion, Jassy gave Ceil a suspicious look, but the older woman was straight-faced. "Maybe that's a good idea. C'mon, Wolfman, let's take care of that cut on your forehead."

Jassy walked toward her trailer, trying not to limp. Her left hip ached where she'd landed on it, and her knee and shin were raw. To her relief, Seth neither commented nor argued, merely followed. But when they entered the trailer, he had plenty to say.

"What the hell is this?" he demanded, indicating the packed saddlebags that she'd left by the door. "You were going to run out on us?"

"I thought about it," she admitted.

"Were you planning on telling anyone? Or were you just going to disappear?"

She neatly avoided answering by saying, "Sit, while I see what I can find in the medicine cabinet."

But when she returned with the first-aid kit, he started in on her again.

"So, are you leaving or what?"

"Or what," she said simply.

Scary though the idea of putting down roots might be, Jassy knew she couldn't do otherwise. She might have come to that conclusion before dawn, but the attack on the refuge and on Seth had forced her decision. Now she was convinced that she belonged at Wolf's Lair with the man she loved.

His belligerent expression relaxed. "So you're going to stay till the end of summer?"

"Longer," she murmured, swabbing Seth's forehead with antiseptic. When she got to the actual cut, he winced. "Sorry. I didn't mean to hurt you."

"Like you never meant to hurt anyone?" Seth asked. "For a pacifist, you certainly can be aggressive. You gave those hoodlums hell."

Trying not to feel guilty about protecting her own, she avoided his eyes and poured antiseptic on another swab. "I couldn't watch anyone being hurt without doing something about it. I told you before, I could take care of myself if I had to. Now hold still while I clean out that cut."

Seth's eyes never left her face. He squinted, however, when she dabbed at the wound.

"But you joined in the fray with such fervor, and with such single-minded purpose. Why was that?"

Wondering if he was teasing her, she gave him an answer that was utterly true. "I don't know what I would have done if anything had happened to you."

"You mean you love me that much?"

"Maybe more," she admitted.

"And you need me?" he prompted.

"I need you."

"About time you admitted you needed someone." Seth grinned and pulled her down into his lap. Though he grunted and winced—his ribs must have bothered him—the sheltering strength of his arms was uncompromising. "Jassy, my love, don't be afraid of The Wolfman."

She ignored the pain shooting through her hip. If she told Seth about it, he might let her go, and she didn't ever want that to happen.

"You're impossible," she murmured, content to nestle against his chest, though careful not to hurt him further.

"We wolf men generally are. But you're the special woman who can handle me."

Sliding a hand to the back of her head, Seth pulled her face close to his. His mouth sought hers with a tenderness she hadn't known he was capable of. Her heart began to pound—not from arousal or excitement, but from the certainty that she was loved. She returned the message wholeheartedly until she heard a wolf howl.

"A-a-w-oo-o-o . . ."

Giggling, Jassy raised her head.

"Oo-o-o-h-h-h . . ."

"A-w-w-w-w . . ."

"Do you think they're howling their approval?" Jassy asked.

"I'd bet on it. They need you, Jassy, just as much as I do," Seth told her. "I promise you won't regret staying. I'm going to make you a real home here." He stroked her cheek and looked at her with such tenderness that she thought she might embarrass herself by crying. "Like all creatures, you need a certain amount of freedom. But even more, you need love and a sense of belonging."

"You've given me what I never dared hoped for, Seth—a place and a reason to put down my roots."

As Seth kissed her again and she heard the wolves singing, Jassy knew she was bound to the earth at last.

Rebels & Rogues

Quinn: He was a real-life hero to everyone except himself.

THE MIGHTY QUINN
by Candace Schuler
Temptation #397, June 1992

All men are not created equal. Some are rough around the edges. Tough-minded but tenderhearted. Incredibly sexy. The tempting fulfillment of every woman's fantasy.

When it's time to fight for what they believe in, to win that special woman, our Rebels and Rogues are heroes at heart. Twelve Rebels and Rogues, one each month in 1992, only from Harlequin Temptation!

❖ *Harlequin*®

JANELLE TAYLOR

Valley of Fire

HARLEQUIN IS PROUD TO PRESENT *VALLEY OF FIRE* BY JANELLE TAYLOR—AUTHOR OF TWENTY-TWO BOOKS, INCLUDING SIX *NEW YORK TIMES* BESTSELLERS

VALLEY OF FIRE—the warm and passionate story of Kathy Alexander, a famous romance author, and Steven Winngate, entrepreneur and owner of the magazine that intended to expose the real Kathy "Brandy" Alexander to her fans.

Don't miss VALLEY OF FIRE, available in May.

OVER THE YEARS, TELEVISION HAS BROUGHT
THE LIVES AND LOVES OF MANY CHARACTERS INTO
YOUR HOMES. NOW HARLEQUIN INTRODUCES YOU
TO THE TOWN AND PEOPLE OF

One small town—twelve terrific love stories.

GREAT READING...GREAT SAVINGS...AND A FABULOUS
FREE GIFT!

Each book set in Tyler is a self-contained love story; together, the
twelve novels stitch the fabric of the community.

By collecting proofs-of-purchase found in each Tyler book, you can
receive a fabulous gift, ABSOLUTELY FREE! And use our special
Tyler coupons to save on your next TYLER book purchase.

Join us for the fourth TYLER book,
MONKEY WRENCH by Nancy Martin.

*Can elderly Rose Atkins successfully bring a new love into
granddaughter Susannah's life?*

"GET AWAY FROM IT ALL" SWEEPSTAKES

HERE'S HOW THE SWEEPSTAKES WORKS

NO PURCHASE NECESSARY

To enter each drawing, complete the appropriate Official Entry Form or a 3" by 5" index card by hand-printing your name, address and phone number and the trip destination that the entry is being submitted for (i.e., Caneel Bay, Canyon Ranch or London and the English Countryside) and mailing it to: Get Away From It All Sweepstakes, P.O. Box 1397, Buffalo, New York 14269-1397.

No responsibility is assumed for lost, late or misdirected mail. Entries must be sent separately with first class postage affixed, and be received by: 4/15/92 for the Caneel Bay Vacation Drawing, 5/15/92 for the Canyon Ranch Vacation Drawing and 6/15/92 for the London and the English Countryside Vacation Drawing. Sweepstakes is open to residents of the U.S. (except Puerto Rico) and Canada, 21 years of age or older as of 5/31/92.

For complete rules send a self-addressed, stamped (WA residents need not affix return postage) envelope to: Get Away From It All Sweepstakes, P.O. Box 4892, Blair, NE 68009.

© 1992 HARLEQUIN ENTERPRISES LTD.   SWP-RLS

"GET AWAY FROM IT ALL" SWEEPSTAKES

HERE'S HOW THE SWEEPSTAKES WORKS

NO PURCHASE NECESSARY

To enter each drawing, complete the appropriate Official Entry Form or a 3" by 5" index card by hand-printing your name, address and phone number and the trip destination that the entry is being submitted for (i.e., Caneel Bay, Canyon Ranch or London and the English Countryside) and mailing it to: Get Away From It All Sweepstakes, P.O. Box 1397, Buffalo, New York 14269-1397.

No responsibility is assumed for lost, late or misdirected mail. Entries must be sent separately with first class postage affixed, and be received by: 4/15/92 for the Caneel Bay Vacation Drawing, 5/15/92 for the Canyon Ranch Vacation Drawing and 6/15/92 for the London and the English Countryside Vacation Drawing. Sweepstakes is open to residents of the U.S. (except Puerto Rico) and Canada, 21 years of age or older as of 5/31/92.

For complete rules send a self-addressed, stamped (WA residents need not affix return postage) envelope to: Get Away From It All Sweepstakes, P.O. Box 4892, Blair, NE 68009.

© 1992 HARLEQUIN ENTERPRISES LTD.   SWP-RLS

"GET AWAY FROM IT ALL"

Brand-new Subscribers-Only Sweepstakes

OFFICIAL ENTRY FORM

This entry must be received by: June 15, 1992
This month's winner will be notified by: June 30, 1992
Trip must be taken between: July 31, 1992—July 31, 1993

YES, I want to win the vacation for two to England. I understand the prize includes round-trip airfare and the two additional prizes revealed in the BONUS PRIZES insert.

Name _____

Address _____

City _____

State/Prov._____ Zip/Postal Code_____

Daytime phone number _____
(Area Code)

Return entries with invoice in envelope provided. Each book in this shipment has two entry coupons — and the more coupons you enter, the better your chances of winning!
© 1992 HARLEQUIN ENTERPRISES LTD.   3M-CPN

"GET AWAY FROM IT ALL"

Brand-new Subscribers-Only Sweepstakes

OFFICIAL ENTRY FORM

This entry must be received by: June 15, 1992
This month's winner will be notified by: June 30, 1992
Trip must be taken between: July 31, 1992—July 31, 1993

YES, I want to win the vacation for two to England. I understand the prize includes round-trip airfare and the two additional prizes revealed in the BONUS PRIZES insert.

Name _____

Address _____

City _____

State/Prov._____ Zip/Postal Code_____

Daytime phone number _____
(Area Code)

Return entries with invoice in envelope provided. Each book in this shipment has two entry coupons — and the more coupons you enter, the better your chances of winning!
© 1992 HARLEQUIN ENTERPRISES LTD.   3M-CPN